'Just Because [We End] Up In Bed Do[esn't Mean] To[gether...]'

Kat said. 'In fact, I ca[n almost guarantee] that it won't.'

'Are you a gambler?' Mac asked.

'I occasionally take a flier on a long shot,' she admitted.

'Okay, what do you think of these odds? I'll help you with your damn research.'

She eyed him with deep suspicion. 'And?'

'And for the time we're together, I'm going to do my damnedest to seduce you, to get you in my bed.'

'And if you don't?'

'Then I have a feeling we'll both be losing.' He stepped closer. 'But I'm betting we end up as lovers. If we do, it's all over when you leave. No regrets.'

'Done,' she said promptly, holding out her hand to seal the bargain.

He took it, tugging her closer.

Then *he* sealed their bargain—with a kiss.

Dear Reader,

While away those long summer evenings with this month's wonderful Silhouette Desires®. August's tall, dark and sexy MAN OF THE MONTH is Calum Tallchief. Cait London's *Tallchief's Bride* follows his quest for the heirloom ring which legend promises will bring him true love...

The romance continues with Cindy Gerard's sensuous *A Bride for Abel Greene*, the next in her NORTHERN LIGHTS BRIDES series, and also with *Roxy and the Rich Man*, the first in a brand new mini-series from Elizabeth Bevarly about brothers and sisters who were separated at birth. The next sibling's story *Lucy and the Loner*, will be on the shelves in November.

You'll love reading about Rebecca Barnett's wild antics as she seduces Raleigh Hanlon in *Rebel's Spirit* by Susan Connell, and there's an emotional and compelling reunion story in *Lovers Only* from Christine Pacheco.

City Girls Need Not Apply is a humorous and delightful novel from one of your favourite award-winning authors—Rita Rainville. Don't miss it!

Have fun!

The Editors

City Girls Need Not Apply

RITA RAINVILLE

™ SILHOUETTE

Desire®

*Silhouette, Silhouette Desire and Colophon
are registered trademarks of Harlequin Books S.A.,
used under licence.*

*First published in Great Britain 1997
Silhouette Books, Eton House, 18-24 Paradise Road,
Richmond, Surrey TW9 1SR*

© Rita Rainville 1997

ISBN 0 373 76056 6

22-9708

*Printed and bound in Great Britain
by Mackays of Chatham PLC, Chatham*

To Lou, a sister in all the important ways

RITA RAINVILLE

has been a favourite with romance readers since the publication of her first book. This award-winning author has always been in love with books—especially romances. In fact, because reading has always been such an important part of her life, she has become a literacy volunteer and now teaches reading to those who have yet to discover the pleasure of a good book.

Other novels by Rita Rainville

Silhouette Desire®

A Touch of Class
Paid in Full
High Spirits
Tumbleweed and Gibraltar
Hot Property
Bedazzled
Husband Material

Silhouette Christmas Stories 1992
'Lights Out!'

A LETTER FROM THE AUTHOR

Dear Reader,

Before Silhouette® bought my first book, I used to wonder how my favourite writers felt when they looked inside their books and saw 'Books by...' followed by a lengthy list of titles.

Well, now I know. They felt a bit surprised and very thrilled.

I have to tell you the surprise and thrill of being a multi-published author will never fade. There is gratitude, as well, for editors who have shared my belief that sexy can also be funny.

But what has made this time so very special is that you, the readers, have written to tell me you fell in love with my heroes and laughed out loud at the zany secondary characters. That was when I realized that you shared the magic of this process with me, and for that I will be forever grateful.

So sit back, take a deep breath and turn the page. The adventure isn't over. There's another romance in the making. And another, and another.

Enjoy!

Rita Rainville

One

"**W**hat the hell are you doing out here in the middle of a storm, you crazy woman!"

Kathryn Wainwright could barely hear her own surprised yelp above the snarling wind. She spun around at the sound of the man's furious roar, almost losing her footing in the ankle-deep snow.

Gasping, she staggered back a couple of steps, momentarily forgetting her misery as she stared in horror at one of the biggest, meanest-looking horses she had ever seen. Her gaze slowly shifted upward and she blinked at the rider through the biting snow. He seemed to match the horse—both in size and temperament.

His scowl and narrowed eyes, which were all Kat could see beneath the wide brim of the cowboy hat, were not comforting. In fact, she reflected with a shudder that was only partly from the cold, it was safe to say that there was not one single thing about man or horse to ease a woman's mind.

Especially a woman who was stranded in the midst of a snowstorm. On foot. In the wilds of Wyoming. Wearing only a ridiculous assortment of summer clothing. Carrying a briefcase. And freezing to death.

The man heaved a sigh. "Come on, let's go."

Kat peered around through the falling snow. Looking back at him, she asked simply, "Where?"

"Up, for starters."

Her gaze met his for a startled second then lowered to the horse. It snorted and shook its head, sending a nasty glob of froth in her direction. Disgusting as it was, she was too cold to do more than clutch her briefcase closer to her chest.

The man nudged the horse nearer and held out a gloved hand to Kat. "Come on."

Kat backed away, shaking her head. "How?" she asked through chattering teeth. "It's too...high."

With an impatient oath, the cowboy slid his snow-covered boot from the stirrup and waggled it. "Step on my foot, grab my hand and swing up behind me."

Kat stared at him blankly as another shudder worked through her. Part of her mind tried to make sense of his directions while another part sluggishly chanted a single word.

Hypothermia.

That was it, she thought, vaguely recalling that she had been reciting all the dismal symptoms of a subnormal body temperature to herself when the man had crept up behind her.

Swearing with a skill that did nothing to relieve his frustration, Mackenzie Ryder shoved his foot back into the stirrup, keeping his gaze on her face, noting the strain in her blue eyes. Eyes so light they seemed almost iridescent. Each time her ridiculously long lashes dropped, she seemed barely able to get them up again.

He leaned over, lifted her as if she weighed no more than a doll and settled her in place before him. It would have been easier without the briefcase, but she clung to it with a determination that told him how bad things were. She wasn't thinking, just moving like a damned robot. Or maybe she couldn't release her fingers from the grip she had on it.

He moved back in the saddle, giving her a few more inches, and before she could slump against him, he tore open his shearling coat. He wrapped the sides around her, hoping the warm fleece lining, as well as his body heat, would penetrate the iciness that encased her. When his hand brushed hers, still grasping the leather case, he muttered, "Here, let me have it."

Her arms tightened convulsively around it and she shook her head. "My...computer," she mumbled.

Mac gave the slim leather case a skeptical look and kneed Red, trusting the gelding to get them home the fastest and safest way. He didn't waste time arguing with the woman—especially about something as stupid as a computer. He had learned a long time ago that the only thing to do with people bordering on hypothermia was to haul their butts in out of the cold and get them warm.

She pressed back against his chest, tremors shaking her nicely rounded body. "That's it, darlin'," he murmured. "Keep shivering. Don't close down on me." More to keep her talking than because he considered the information vital, Mac nudged her with his shoulder. "So, what are you doing out here?"

"My car...broke down."

"Engine trouble?"

She shook her head. "Ditch," she enunciated carefully. "My car slid in."

Mac briefly closed his eyes. Of course it had. It was exactly what any little red sports car owned by a city girl would do in weather like this. Slide in a ditch. He opened his eyes and frowned down through the swirling snowflakes at the dark hair brushing against his chin. She didn't even have the sense to wear a hat. Or put on gloves.

His scowl deepened as he muttered a simple request that could have been a prayer or an oath. "God protect me from city girls." Lost lambs in the wilderness—just like his wife had been. And ignorance could kill them—just as it had killed his wife. Cynthia hadn't had a fighting chance, and this one wouldn't, either—if left on her own.

He could spot one a mile away. Of course, in the case of the woman pressing back against his chest and sharing his coat, it had been easier than usual. Everything had pointed to the obvious conclusion.

As far as he could tell, the only sensible thing she'd done was tap out a distress signal on her car horn every few seconds before she'd decided to hoof it. Even so, if he had been in the house instead of heading in that direction from the pasture, he'd never have heard it.

The car, tilted headfirst in the shallow ditch, had been a dead giveaway. No one around here would tackle the rutted dirt road with a low-slung toy like that. Her partially covered tracks had been the next clue. Shoes, with a defined low heel, not boots. He glanced down and shook his head at her footgear. Leather loafers and ankle socks.

It figured.

By the time he'd caught up with her, he'd been ready for almost anything—even the sight of a woman wearing several layers of light clothes, clutching an expensive leather briefcase to her chest and soliloquizing about hypothermia. She had been so intent on the one-sided conversation she hadn't even heard him come up behind her.

"Why here?" he persisted. "Why on this road?" It was a good question. The road broke off the main artery several miles back and dead-ended at his house. He couldn't think of one logical reason why a woman claiming she was carrying a computer in a briefcase would be trudging up the road to his place in the middle of a storm. Or, for that matter, why she'd be doing it, period—whatever the weather.

Especially a woman like this one. Even with her wet hair hanging like a dark curtain around her face, a face that was almost as white as the falling snow, her looks would stop most men dead in their tracks.

Taken feature by feature, she wasn't beautiful, he decided, shifting her closer. The thought didn't comfort him. Even if she wasn't drop-dead gorgeous, he wasn't off the hook, not by a long shot. Because, although dazed and half-frozen, she'd given him one lost look and almost had him falling off Red.

Tightening his knees, he urged the gelding along. Part of the problem, he admitted disgustedly, was that he had been without a woman for too long. Another part was that he was a sucker for lost lambs. And he suspected that when this particular lamb thawed out, she'd be as sexy as hell. On top of that, he genuinely liked women. He liked their softness, their fragrance, their laughter, everything about them. Feeling that way, he found life hell without them, but living with guilt and regret was even worse.

Mac grimly tightened his arm around her waist when she shivered, grateful that she was too miserable to realize what her shapely bottom, sliding against him with every step Red took, was doing to him.

"Why here?" he repeated, tugging at the lapel of his jacket in an attempt to protect her face. Another shiver was her only response.

Mac gave up and urged Red past the barn to the back stairs of the house. In one lithe movement he stepped down, dropped the reins and hauled her into his arms. Shouldering through the door, he stamped the snow from his boots in the small enclosed porch and opened the kitchen door. "Claude?" His roar echoed down the hallway. "Davy? Come here."

He had eased her to her feet and was steadying her when his cook entered with a limp that spoke volumes about cold weather and arthritic knees, followed closely by his son.

Claude rested a gnarled hand on the woman's shoulder, squeezing lightly and smiled at her. "Well, what've we got here? What's your name, honey?"

Mac scowled. "You can be sociable later. Crank up the heat in here and get her into a warm bath. I've got to take care of Red."

Kat licked her lips. "Kat," she said, gazing straight into the old man's eyes. "With a *K*."

Mac's scowl darkened. "Move it," he commanded. "*Now.* Davy, help her off with her shoes and socks while Claude gets the water going in the tub." He turned and went back through the door as Claude's soft voice encouraged their guest.

"Okay, Kat with a *K*, let's get you warmed up. That's the ticket, girl, straight down the hall here and up the stairs. Me and Davy'll fix you up just fine."

An hour later Kat swiped at the steamy bathroom mirror with her towel, wincing at the image gazing back at her. Today had definitely not been one of her better days. She had been inexcusably careless, especially for someone who was supposed to be so bright.

Pathetic, she decided, pulling her hair back and studying her face. And grim. Enough to give that sober little kid, Davy, nightmares. Maybe not, though. Maybe the state of Wyoming produced a tough breed—men to match the mountains—and started early with the little ones. Davy had certainly been efficient enough when he'd nudged her down

on the wide edge of the tub and removed her shoes and
socks while the old man, Claude, started running the water.

Davy had pulled down the zipper of her jacket and
tugged it off. He'd matter-of-factly unbuttoned her outer
blouse and frowned worriedly when she'd held out her hand
to stop him and insisted that she could do the rest. After
directing her to toss her clothes out into the hall, he'd reluctantly followed the old man out the door. In between
shudders, she had eventually completed the task, bundling
up everything except her underwear.

She let her hair fall back around her face, smiling, remembering how Davy had returned a few minutes later,
knocking politely and asking if she needed anything. Even
later, he'd knocked again, telling her he was leaving her
some clothes by the door.

Kat turned the knob and peered out cautiously. The
promised pile of clothing was almost at her feet. Snatching
them up, she closed the door and turned to examine her
loot.

Walking downstairs a few minutes later, Kat tugged self-
consciously at the tight jeans. It didn't take a certified genius—even though that was precisely what she was—to
figure out that she was wearing Claude's clothing. He was
her height—five foot six inches—give or take an inch, and
his T-shirt, flannel shirt and heavy white cotton socks were
a comfortable fit. The jeans were another story.

After stopping on the landing to do a couple of deep
knee bends, Kat ran a hand across the taut fabric that covered her bottom and sighed. Thinking longingly of the
roomy, pleated slacks she had turned over to Davy, she
went down the rest of the stairs to the dining room and
looked around.

The room showed no signs of a woman's touch. The
round oak table and chairs were of good quality, but built
for service rather than esthetics. The matching sideboard

was piled high with pamphlets and papers. She trailed into the living room and found more of the same. The rooms were clean, furniture well kept, but it was definitely a man's house. No flowers, no knickknacks, and any pictures on the light, paneled walls were of horses. The magazines piled on all the flat surfaces featured ranches, cows and more horses.

Turning back, Kat followed the sound of conversation and stopped at the swinging kitchen door. It was open, and she stopped, suddenly aware that she had almost walked in on a private conversation.

"She's real pretty, isn't she, Claude?" Davy asked in a thoughtful voice. His back was to the door, and Kat found herself wishing she could see his expression.

The older man looked up from the chunks of meat and onion sizzling in a large skillet. He spotted Kat looking indecisive and winked at her, jerking his head in a silent invitation to join them.

"Yep, she is that, Davy boy. Even froze up like a snowball, she's a looker."

"Was my mother that pretty?"

Claude looked down at the pile of vegetables on the cutting board, drawing them together with the edge of his knife. "You've seen pictures of her. What do *you* think?"

Davy nodded. "Her hair was lighter, but she was pretty."

Past tense, Kat reflected. That didn't sound good for Davy. Stepping into the room, she absently noted that its stark cleanliness matched the rest of the house. Wherever Davy's mother was, she definitely wasn't around here. Her attention switched to the two males, one young, one old, both looking at her expectantly.

"Well, here are my two favorite people," she said brightly. "Heroes, both of you. I'll never forget the men who thawed me out."

Davy studied her with serious brown eyes. "What about my daddy?"

Tilting her head, Kat smiled at him. "What about your daddy?"

"He brought you to the house. Is he one of your favorite people, too?"

Deep down, Kat wasn't surprised. It was logical that Davy should belong to her rescuer. Claude was obviously too old to be the father. It was just hard to believe that the same genes ran through the iron man on the horse and this cute little sobersides.

She nodded. "Well, if he did that, I suppose he's a hero, too."

"And he's a favored person?" Davy persisted.

Claude snorted and turned back to his stew makings. His white hair was closely cropped, and he moved his wiry body with the impatient energy of a once-active man held back by age and arthritis. His jeans hung around his scrawny hips.

"Fair's fair," Kat said with a sigh. "I guess so."

"Good." Davy nodded with satisfaction.

Vigorously rinsing his hands, Claude looked over his shoulder at them. "Sit down, Kat with a *K,* and I'll get you a cup of coffee."

Kat moved obediently to the table, taking a seat across from Davy. "You don't happen to have some hot water and a tea bag floating around, do you?"

"No problem a-tall," he drawled. While he splashed water in a pan and set it on one of the burners of the electric stove, Davy got up and walked around the table, stopping before Kat.

Holding out his hand, he said solemnly, "I'm Davy Ryder. I'm six, my mama's in heaven and Miss Tedley, my teacher, says I'm more trouble than a handful of hornets."

"No kidding," she responded lightly, resisting the impulse to ruffle his hair. "I imagine most people wouldn't agree with her." Kat took his small hand in hers and gave it the businesslike shake he seemed to expect, hiding the anger that welled up inside her. What she wanted to do with both her hands was wrap them around the neck of his irresponsible teacher and squeeze. Hard. Instead, she looked into his clear, innocent eyes and smiled. And fell a little bit in love.

He was a darling brown boy. Brown eyes, anxious to please, soft skin tanned by the sun, and hair the color of brewed coffee that sprouted from a cowlick on his crown and fell over his brow. In about ten years, anxious fathers would be installing chains on their daughters' bedroom doors and keeping their shotguns handy, she thought after another look at his slim face, straight little nose and well-shaped lips.

The expectant look in Davy's eyes reminded her that she had gotten sidetracked. "My name is Kathryn—"

"With a *K*," he interjected soberly.

She nodded. "Right. Kathryn Wainwright. But I hope you'll call me Kat, because that's the name my friends use." His smile, when it came, was well worth waiting for, she decided. "I'm twenty-nine, and I live and work in Denver."

"And I'm Claude." The old man plunked a mug down on the table before her. "Used to be the foreman around here. Now I'm the chief cook and bottle washer." He waited for Davy to return to his place, then took the chair next to his and gazed at her curiously. "So, Kat, what are you doing in our neck of the woods?"

"I've been wondering that myself."

The deep voice of the man behind her was one not easily forgotten, Kat reflected. She had heard it in everything between a whisper and a roar. After plunking her in front of him on the saddle, he'd kept his mouth near her ear, talking

in a comforting, laid-back drawl that made the freezing trip
to the house seem bearable. For the most part she'd had no
idea what he'd said, but she had felt the vibrations in his
chest against her back and had been soothed. Kat set her
mug on the table and turned to face her rescuer.

Good grief, she thought inadequately as she drew in a
long breath. Davy's daddy cleans up real nice. He lounged
in the doorway, a bigger, tougher, harder version of his son,
obviously waiting for her reply. She took her time. He had
the same thick, coffee-colored hair as his son, only his was
brushed back and badly in need of a haircut. His brown
eyes were a shade darker and not nearly as anxious to
please. His expression was blatantly male—appreciative
and coolly assessing at the same time.

Something about his stance reminded Kat of the feeling
she had had on the ride to the house—a feeling that had
seeped through the cold and weariness and his honey-warm
drawl. It had been the overwhelming impression that her
rescuer had been royally ticked off.

At her.

And despite his sizzling gaze, she realized that he still
felt that way. There was definitely an edge to that look. She
wondered about it briefly before deciding that there was
simply no accounting for a person's reaction. Even hers,
right now. It was nerves, she decided, rubbing her damp
palms on her jeaned thighs. Or the residual effects of nearly
freezing to death. She certainly wasn't attracted to him. No,
it definitely wasn't attraction.

His hair was damp from his shower, and he wore a blue
work shirt and jeans, both white at the stress points from
innumerable washings. The soft fabric followed the con-
tours of his broad shoulders, narrow hips and muscular
thighs. If Miss Tedley thought the son was trouble, she
obviously hadn't taken a good look at the father, Kat decided, deliberately shifting her gaze back to Claude.

"What am I doing here?" she hedged, wondering how to explain the complicated series of events that had led to her present situation. She opted for the most convenient explanation. It had the advantage of being at least partly true, and since she would be leaving tomorrow there was no reason to even mention her job. "I'm on vacation. On my way to Yellowstone."

She felt the silence behind her, as if the man was processing her response, probing for hidden messages. Before he could arrive at a conclusion, Kat smoothly changed the subject.

"I owe you a lot, Mr. Ryder," she said, glancing up as he moved into the room on stockinged feet and stopped at the table. "If you hadn't rescued me, I doubt if I'd be planning a vacation at Yellowstone or anywhere else. Thank you. I don't know what I would have done—"

"Mac."

Kat stopped. "What?"

"The name's Mackenzie," he said softly. "Mac will do."

"Oh." She gave a small shrug. "Okay. Well, thank you very much, Mac."

"You're welcome."

"You're a hero, Daddy."

Mac's brows rose and he grinned down at his son. "Oh? Says who?"

"Kat. She said you're a favored person," Davy told him complacently.

"Is that so?" He turned toward Kat and watched with interest as her cheeks pinkened. She shot him a disgruntled look, and he grinned again. "I imagine it's the first and last time I'll make that list." Moving with a swiftness that made Kat blink, he hauled Davy up into his arms, flipped him over and, holding him by his skinny ankles, let him dangle upside down.

At Davy's delighted shout of laughter, Kat relaxed, her vague concern for the boy easing. If the way he whacked at Mac's legs was any indication, she thought, the horseplay was a familiar pattern. Beneath his sober exterior, Davy was just a little boy who loved to screech and roughhouse with his dad. She watched the two of them thoughtfully, considering the amazing transformation a mere smile could make in a hostile man.

"Yellowstone, huh?" Claude regarded her over the rim of his mug. "You looked more like you were dressed for Hawaii."

Kat grimaced. "A slight miscalculation on my part. When I left Colorado, it was hot. I should have known that the weather could be just as unpredictable here as it is there. When I leave tomorrow, I'll have to buy some heavier things."

Mac gave Davy another bone-rattling shake and elicited another delighted shriek. He looked at Kat and shook his head. "Unless you can salvage what you had on, count on wearing Claude's things for a few days."

"Why?" Kat turned to face him, then wished she hadn't. His quick glance was unsettling.

"Do you ever listen to the radio in that fancy car of yours?"

"Of course I do. I almost always have it on."

"Were you listening today?"

She shook her head slowly, stiffening at the sound of his sweeter-than-honey drawl. "I was playing tapes."

"So you didn't hear any weather reports?"

Kat groaned. "I don't think I want to hear this."

"A full-fledged storm," Mac confirmed, setting Davy on his feet with surprising gentleness. "They expect it to last a couple of days. Add another day for the roads to be plowed and your car checked and—"

"And I've got big trouble," Kat said glumly.

"Hell, Kat, there's no problem on our side," Claude said genially. "Just consider this part of your vacation."

Davy nodded in agreement, hope and excitement making his eyes bright. "There won't be any school, and we can play cards."

Mac, she noted, wasn't exactly a font of encouraging words. Nor was he hauling out the welcome mat. The quick look he shot her made his feelings crystal clear. He didn't want her here—not in his house, not on his ranch and probably not in the same county.

"Come on, Davy," he said abruptly. "I've got some things to do upstairs. You can help me." Davy nodded agreeably and dashed out the door.

Kat's expression was thoughtful when she turned to Claude. "Is it something I said, or does he treat all women this way?"

Claude made a neutral sound as he swallowed the last of his coffee. "What way?" he finally asked, cupping the mug with his hands.

"Like we have the plague."

"Don't take it personal." He got up and made a production of scooping the vegetables into the boiling meat broth and looking for a lid to match the pan. "Mac's wife died out there," he said nodding in the direction of the window, "in a storm like this. Of exposure. Not too long after Davy was born." He turned, taking in Kat's appalled expression. "Times like these, he does a lot of rememberin'. Makes him madder 'n hell to see a woman out in weather like this."

Kat's sigh was replete with self-disgust. "Especially if she's dressed for a picnic."

"Yup."

"So what do I do, try to stay out of sight until the storm's over?"

"Nah." He slammed the lid on the pot and turned down

the fire. "Relax. Davy'll enjoy your company—and Mac? He'll come around. Eventually."

"Good night, Claude. Thanks again for everything."
"See you in the mornin', Kat. Might as well sleep in if you can."

She sighed as he hobbled out the door, heading for his room by the kitchen. Mac and Davy had left a few minutes earlier, and she was alone.

At last.

Kat gazed idly around the large, silent living room, wondering if she should go up to the bedroom Davy had shown her after dinner. She knew instantly that she wouldn't. Not until she'd settled down. And there was no doubt about who had upset her, who had shrunk the ample room to claustrophobic proportions. Mackenzie Ryder, with his sharp eyes and softly drawled words.

He'll come around. Eventually.

She thought of Claude's words and decided she didn't want the man coming around. Ever.

Mac played merry hell with a woman's nervous system, she reflected glumly. His hot, steady gaze, following her every move, had become even more apparent when the storm had cut off the television. He was more male than any man had a right to be, and if the expression in his eyes was any indication, he was bristling with heat, hunger and hormones.

And he wanted her.

He didn't know anything about her, apparently didn't even *like* her, but he wanted her. And each of them in the room—at least the three adults—had been aware of the fact. She had caught Claude grinning every now and then, looking pleased as punch. Davy's puzzled glances had bounced back and forth between them, obviously aware of the tension but finding no explanation. Mac had grown increasingly grim with each passing minute, and she had been ready to bolt back out into the storm.

All right, she admitted crossly as she curled up in the corner of the couch, so he looked like something out of a hunk-of-the-month publication. There were a lot of drop-dead-gorgeous men in the world. Some of them also wore cowboy hats and did things to jeans and work shirts that were positively indecent. Some of them had similar killer smiles. So what?

So she had never dealt with one before.

So maybe her mother's lectures on advancing age, using one's brains for something beside work and predictions of a lonely life were getting to her.

So maybe he didn't look like anybody's daddy and was a far cry from the cerebral type she usually dated.

So it didn't matter. She was not going to play Jane to his Tarzan—or the cowboy equivalent, whatever that was. She wasn't going to play anything except safe. She would stick like glue to Davy and let his deadly daddy handle his own problems.

Cheered by her self-directed pep talk, Kat got up and headed for the stairs, turning off the lamp as she went. She had just reached her door and was wondering if they left on the muted hall light for Davy when Mac stepped out of the boy's room. His unbuttoned shirt hung open, displaying a thatch of dark brown hair on his broad chest. His glittering gaze was hot and direct.

"I was just, uh, turning in," she said breathlessly, grabbing for the knob. "Good night."

Uh-oh. Trouble. *Big* trouble. Her mind chattered a red alert as several long, lazy strides brought him beside her. Mac stopped and clamped his hands on the jamb, caging her against the door.

He was too close, too big, too warm. She could feel his heat radiating outward, covering her like a down blanket as she reached behind her and fumbled with the knob. She froze, her breath cutting off when Mac bent his head.

"Hell," he muttered. "Why don't we just get this over with?" When she gazed at him, speechless, he brushed his lips over hers.

"Over?" Kat croaked, stunned by his touch.

"Yeah." He kissed the corner of her mouth, savoring her. "We both know it's going to happen sooner or later. So let's just get it behind us, okay? Then we don't have to worry about it." His lips settled on hers again, stopping any arguments.

About to protest, Kat forgot what she was going to say when he wrapped his arms around her and pulled her against him. His kiss was like a drug, luring her closer, into heat and darkness, to a dizzying world of pure sensation.

Kat wound her arms around his neck, linking her fingers at his nape. Her sigh was a soft sound of satisfaction. And encouragement. She nestled closer, absorbing the smell of him—soap and pure male. When Mac's fingers worked down her spine she went lax, letting him support her weight.

He groaned, and the vibration she felt deep in her chest sparked a matching hunger. Shaking, she lowered her arms and wrapped them around his waist beneath his shirt, flattening her palms against the warm skin on his back.

At the touch of flesh against flesh, Mac jerked convulsively and raised his head. He closed his eyes briefly and swore, a soft, sibilant Anglo-Saxon oath. A second later his hands clamped on her shoulders and he stepped back.

"Dammit, Kat, I didn't mean to—"

She held up her hand, stopping him, too rattled to think, much less talk. Shaking her head, she finally turned the knob behind her and backed into her room. He braced one hand against the door to keep it open while he pulled something out of the pocket of his jeans.

He held it out to her. When she automatically offered her hand, he dropped a skeleton key in her palm and closed her fingers around it.

"Lock your door," he said tersely, then he turned and strode down the hall to his room.

Two

Several hours later, Kat, still wearing Claude's donated clothes, eased down the dark stairway, her right hand trailing the oak banister, her left holding the slim, state-of-the-art computer to her breast. Once she was settled in Mac's office where she wouldn't disturb anyone, she estimated that she could get several hours work done.

Well, at least one question about the house had been answered, she thought wryly. They did not leave on a light for Davy. The other questions she'd been brooding about—the weather, her project timeline and skunks—were still up in the air.

Just as she passed the grandfather clock on the landing, it struck one, shattering the silence of the night. She jumped and clung to the railing, pressing the computer to her thudding heart.

"Stupid," she muttered when her racing pulse finally steadied and she began feeling her way down the steps again. "This is really stupid." She was certain that if given the choice, Mac would rather have a guest turn on the lights than break a leg in the dark, but sheer instinct kept her moving forward.

Three hours of tossing and turning had finally convinced her that she wasn't going to sleep. Since she was normally a night owl, accustomed to working late hours, she wasn't surprised, but she had thought that a near-fatal incident might possibly result in an earlier night. Obviously it hadn't. But that was her problem and no reason to disturb anyone else. Especially Mac.

Davy or Claude would have been welcome company, helping to pass away the restless hours. Mac, with hunger burning in his dark eyes, was a different story. He was trouble looking for a place to happen, and she had to face the fact that she was vulnerable.

Her mother was right, she reflected with a sigh. Persistent as a mosquito and annoying, but right. She had been wrapped up in her work for too long. She couldn't even remember when she had broken off her lukewarm relationship with Brian. Months ago, somewhere around last Christmas. And since then, there had been nothing but work.

Kat eased her foot forward and gave a sigh of satisfaction when she felt the living room carpet beneath her stockinged feet. Winding her way through the furniture as she headed for the smaller room where Mac did his work, she switched her mental gears from the lackluster past and thought about her host. Disturbing him would be a bit like rousing a grizzly. Maybe even worse.

No, making herself invisible was the best solution, she reflected, moving quietly across the room. Mac had not given her the key to her room because he was worried about robbers or rustlers. His concern was a matter of control—or lack of it—and after that sizzling kiss in the hall, it wasn't surprising. What *had* been a shock was to find that her control was no better than his.

Kat stopped in her tracks, blinking, when she realized that Mac must have put the key in his pocket early in the evening, long *before* they had kissed. Deciding to consider the ramifications of that later, she moved again, heading for the door of the comfortable room that housed Mac's huge desk and a game table for Davy. It was closed, with a strip of light seeping through the bottom.

She opened the door a crack and peeked inside. Davy sat cross-legged on the floor, a small silhouette against the flames in the fireplace. Stepping into the cozy room, Kat silently closed the door behind her. "Hi, kiddo. What are you doing up so late?"

Davy looked up with a shy smile. "Playing cards."

A literal child, Kat reflected, returning his smile. She set the computer on the sofa and settled on the floor across from him, studying the solitaire game spread out between them. "Looks like you're stuck."

"Yeah. It's my sixth game and I haven't won yet."

"Do you ever cheat?"

His lashes lifted and he slanted a glance at her. Apparently deciding that the question hadn't been a test, he shook his head. "Nope. Then it wouldn't be any fun."

A young man after her own heart, Kat decided. "I assume you're working on the theory of no pain, no gain?"

He grinned and ducked his head. "Yeah."

"Doesn't your dad worry about you doing this?" When he glanced up, puzzled, she added, "Building a fire and playing cards in the middle of the night?"

He shook his head again. "Daddy says it's okay. As long as I'm responsible. And careful. He taught me how to take care of the fire." He paused, then seemed to think she needed more assurance. "Daddy and Claude need more sleep than I do," he confided, "so they can't get up with me when I'm not sleepy."

"Do you do this every night?"

Davy checked the cards one last time before he gave up. "Almost."

Watching him painstakingly scoop up the cards and shuffle them, she was struck by the familiarity of the scene. As a child, she had spent many nights just like this, keeping herself busy while her exhausted parents slept.

"Do you know how to play rummy?" Kat asked, leaning back against a sturdy oak chair.

"Gin or the other kind?"

"Either."

"Yeah." His eyes brightened. "You wanna play?"

Kat grinned. "I'm considering it."

"In that case I'd rather play my favorite game."

"What's that?"

"Strip poker."

Kat eyed him narrowly, but he looked up at her as innocent as the proverbial lamb. Maybe it was a genetic thing with male Ryders, she reflected, remembering the expression in Mac's eyes before he'd left her with the key. Or maybe it was simply a male thing, and Davy was starting early. "Who taught you how to play that?" she asked, keeping her tone light and fervently hoping that the answer was one she could live with.

"Daddy. We play it sometimes at night when I'm not tired. If I get down to my jeans, I have to get my pajamas on and go to bed."

"Ah." The sound was a combination of relief and encouragement. "And what happens if you win?"

"I get to stay up an extra hour."

She rolled her eyes. "Dare I ask who wins the most?"

Davy grinned. "It's about even, but I think sometimes he cheats."

"Okay, kid. Let's see how good you really are. Deal me in."

"Strip poker?" he asked hopefully.

"No way. Rummy. The other kind." This time she did lean over and ruffle his hair. "I'm not losing my clothes to a six-year-old. Besides, Claude might not like me being so careless with his britches."

"They look a lot better on you than they do on him," Davy commented, giving them a long, assessing glance before carefully dealing the cards.

Yes, Kat thought with a sigh. Innocent or not, he was his father's son.

At the end of the third game, which she won by a narrow margin by adopting Davy's cutthroat tactics, Kat scooped up the cards and began shuffling. "Okay, that's two for you and one for me. Do you know how to play blackjack?"

Davy blinked. "The one where you try to make twenty-one?"

"That's the one."

"Yep."

"Let's give it a try."

"What'll we use for money?"

She pointed to the pencil and paper at her side. "We'll just mark down how many times we win. Ready? Here goes."

She kept the game moving at a brisk pace, never cutting Davy any slack, smiling when he kept up with her. Little Davy, she reflected as she dealt, was more than a charmer. He was six-going-on-thirty, and if she was any judge, brilliant. And he counted cards like a pro. Almost as well as she did.

"Davy, my lad, if it wasn't against the law, I'd pack you up and take you to Vegas. With your innocent eyes and my legs, we'd make a killing."

One side of his mouth kicked up. "Is that a good thing?"

"As long as we're not talking about physical violence, it's an excellent thing." Kat tossed the cards in a heap between them and pulled Davy over on her lap. Giving him a hug, she said, "Do you like books?"

He nodded against her shoulder.

"What kind?"

"The kind I read, and the kind people read to me."

"A man of discriminating taste," she said dryly.

Davy giggled. "What kind do you like?"

"All kinds. As long as they have words, I'll read them. Tell you what, go get two books, one you can read to me and one for me to read to you." She watched him pad over to the bookshelves and silently study the titles within his reach. Mac kept a well-stocked library, she noted idly. One of the lower shelves bristled with children's books that she recognized from reading sessions with her nephew. The others ranged from encyclopedias and reference material to biographies and fiction, with an emphasis on mysteries.

While Davy debated, she moved to the leather couch and sank into the soft cushions, tucking the computer out of harm's way. The work she had intended to do tonight could wait, she reflected. What she was doing was far more important.

When Davy returned, he climbed up next to her, sighing when her arm dropped around his narrow shoulders and tugged him closer. He looked up at her. "Who reads first?"

"You do. I'll close my eyes and listen." Kat leaned back, resting her head against a colorful afghan, smiling faintly at his sober little voice and wondering about his selections. He'd had to stretch to reach them. The book he'd plopped into her lap was an adventure story, an adult fiction.

So was the one Davy was reading.

Close to dawn, Mac moved lightly down the stairs, fully dressed except for his boots. He carried them, a habit he'd formed when Davy was born and had never broken. It was still black outside. Dark and surly as his mood, he admitted silently.

He hadn't slept worth a damn—tossed and turned all night, thinking about Kat just two rooms down the hall. He'd known the second he'd seen her that she was trouble. And if he'd had any doubts, one look at her in Claude's jeans had convinced him. The damned pants clung tighter than a second skin, showing every inch of her endless legs and shaping her bottom like a lover's hands.

He wanted her. There wasn't a square inch on his body that didn't ache from wanting. Hell, what he needed to do was walk out in the snow and sit until he cooled off. And that would work about as long as it took to dry off, then he'd be right back where he started, he decided in disgust.

The kiss. That had been a mistake. A big one. Let's get it over with, he'd told her. Then we don't have to worry about it. Anyone with a single brain cell should have know it wouldn't work that way. Not when all he wanted to do was taste her, feel her warm, sweet body against his. Not when she responded like a woman who wanted—and needed—a man.

No, what he really needed to do was take a trip out of town and visit Lena Gray for a few days. He and Lena had a lot in common. They were friends, neither wanted to get married and they both had needs. They enjoyed being together and didn't miss each other when they were apart. It had been too long—months—since he'd seen her.

That was his problem, he reflected, heading for his office. Hormones getting out of hand. It had nothing to do with Kat Wainwright. Nothing at all.

He saw the slit of light beneath the office door and shook his head. Davy. Squashing the familiar tide of guilt that hit him, he set down his boots and turned the knob. Davy was fine, he told himself grimly. He had weird sleeping habits, but he was fine. He was well adjusted and happy, and that was the main thing. So what if he fell asleep down here, Mac thought, silently opening the door. He did it all the time.

Mac stopped as if he had run into a wall, and stared at the couch. Yeah, Davy made a habit of it, all right, but not like this. He had never fallen asleep snuggled next to a woman, his bottom tucked against her stomach. Even though they were covered with the afghan, Mac could see the shape of Kat's arm around his son, holding him in her sleep. Her dark cloud of hair tumbled over his shoulders like a lustrous blanket, and Davy had a lock caught between his fingers, as if he had been stroking it as he'd fallen asleep.

A shaft of pure envy shot through Mac as he walked to the sofa and looked down at them, and he knew he'd give a lot—a hell of a lot—to change places with his son. His body tightened in agreement as he seriously considered doing just that, but he shook his head and slowly let out his pent-up breath. People had called Mackenzie Ryder a lot of things, but no one had ever called him stupid. And thoughts like that were not only stupid, they were dangerous.

Nudging a book aside with his foot, Mac peeled back the afghan and gently untangled Davy from Kat's embrace. "Come on, cowboy," he murmured, lifting him up and tucking the cover back around Kat. "Let's get you in bed."

Davy murmured a sleepy protest then rubbed his cheek on Mac's shoulder and went slack. He didn't move when Mac climbed the stairs, and he slid out of Mac's arms and into his own bed without a sound.

With every step Mac took back down the stairs, he told himself that he was going out to the barn. He'd already forgotten what he had wanted in the office, now he would forget that Kat was sprawled on the couch, warm and inviting. He'd go to the barn, freeze his butt off and take care of the horses.

"The hell I will," he muttered, backtracking to the office.

She hadn't moved. He rested his hands on his hips and looked down at her. He had spent an evening watching her, and he decided again that his first impression had been right. She wasn't beautiful. Or rather, she didn't have the distant, unapproachable kind of beauty that models strove for.

What she had was even better. Dark hair alive with red and gold highlights and eyes that tilted slightly at the corners. Eyes that could glitter with frost or smile when she looked at Davy. A small straight nose, a generous mouth and a softly pointed chin that could definitely be classified as stubborn.

She was dangerously tempting, and she was going to be sharing his house for at least three days.

"Okay, sweetheart, let's get you to bed." He scooped her up, cover and all, and headed toward the room she hadn't bothered to lock. Kat made the same soft sound Davy had made, then snuggled closer, resting her head on Mac's shoulder.

He took his time on the stairs, enjoying the soft curves pressed against him. Shouldering open her door, he hit the light switch with his elbow and gazed at the rumpled bed.

"Looks like you didn't have any better luck sleeping than I did," he murmured as he crossed the room and balanced one knee on the mattress while he eased her down. His plan—to cover her and leave—changed when she slid her arms around his neck and threaded her fingers through his hair. Instead, he listened to his pulsing body and sat beside her, his hip nudging hers, then caged her by planting a hand on either side of her shoulders, and settled back to see what the fates were offering.

Kat opened her eyes and blinked sleepily at him. "You gave me a key."

"You didn't use it."

Her brows drew together in a frown. "You carried me up here?"

"Yep."

"Shouldn't have. I'm heavy."

"Not compared to a bale of hay." Amusement cooled his overheated hormones. There was going to be no seduction scene tonight. She obviously slept as heavily as his son, and he'd been through this too many times with Davy to be mistaken. Kat might have her eyes open, but she wasn't awake. He waited, wondering what else she'd say while her defenses were down.

"I don't have time," she murmured, her eyelids drooping.

"For what?"

"You. Any sexy man. Have to work."

"What's the rush?"

Kat sighed. "They'll go to sleep. Have to find them first." Her lashes lifted and she slid her fingers through his hair, stopping to touch a questing thumb to his earlobe. "Davy's a delicious boy."

Mac grinned. "Thank you, ma'am."

"Welcome. So are you."

"Delicious?"

"Yeah. But trouble. Like hornets."

"So are you, darlin', so are you."

Kat didn't hear him. Her lax hands slid down his chest and came to rest at her waist. Her eyes closed and she was gone. Mac gazed down at her, his oath barely a sound in the silent room. Fighting loneliness was hard enough at the best of times. Hard work and keeping so busy he didn't have time to think usually worked, but it wasn't always the answer.

Like right now.

Sometimes the need caught him by surprise.

Like right now.

The last thing he wanted was to be snowbound with a city girl with laughing eyes who was falling for his son. His mouth grimly set, he tucked the covers around her and got to his feet. As he turned off the light and closed the door, he shook his head ruefully, wondering how much of the conversation she'd remember tomorrow.

"Well, I took your advice and slept in." Kat stood in the kitchen doorway and watched Claude splashing vigorously in soapy water at the sink. She had washed, done what she could with her limited wardrobe and decided she couldn't stall any longer.

Her recollection of last night was quite clear—up to the point where she'd fallen asleep holding Davy. She had a vague impression that sometime later Mac had carried her upstairs to bed. Beyond that, everything was mercifully erased. Her fervent wish was that Mac had left immediately. Barring that, she could only hope that she hadn't indulged in one of her infamous sleep-talking sessions. Her family's evaluation of her nocturnal conversations was quite clear—she lost all sense of prudence and was devastatingly honest. That, she reflected glumly, was not the state to be in when talking with Mac.

"I guess I really needed the sleep."

"There you go," Claude said approvingly. "How about some breakfast?"

"I'll just make some tea."

He made a disgusted sound and eyed her as if he suspected she might keel over on the floor. "Live on that stuff long enough and you won't even cast a shadow. At least have a piece of coffee cake.'' He pointed to a square pan with his elbow. ''Fresh made this morning.''

Kat leaned over to take a closer look and inhaled appreciatively. ''Omigod.'' She looked at him with awe. ''It's got cinnamon and nuts and little crumbly things.''

''Brown sugar, butter and oats.''

''You did this?''

Claude snorted. '''Course I did. You won't find none a that store-bought stuff in *my* kitchen. Has all the taste of a cardboard box.''

''Where's a knife?'' Kat demanded, turning to face him. She decided not to tell him that she lived on ''store-bought'' stuff. ''And a plate.''

''Now you're talkin'. The drawer by your hip pocket and the cupboard right in front of you.''

''Grab a plate for me, too,'' Mac said from somewhere behind her.

Kat's hand stilled on the saucers. Drat the man. He crept around like a shadow, bobbing up without so much as clearing his throat. ''Sure. Want me to heat the coffee?''

''I always keep some hot in a thermos.''

''No, thanks. I'll get it.''

The two men spoke at the same time, and Kat concentrated on the cake while Mac reached over her shoulder for a mug. She felt the heat from his body, and it made her mildly claustrophobic. ''Claude, you want a piece?''

''Nah.'' He hastily dried his hands and tossed the towel on the sink. ''I gotta go, uh, go…dust the furniture. Yeah, that's it, I gotta dust.''

''Place looks fine to me,'' Mac said blandly, pouring the strong coffee.

Claude made a disgusted sound. ''Since when were you a judge? We could have an inch of fuzz on every table and you'd never even notice.'' He grabbed an oily cloth from beneath the sink and stomped out of the room, leaving the swinging door flapping behind him.

Mac sat across from Kat, sipping his coffee, while she dug into the cake. "Claude was being subtle," he mentioned just as she popped a piece in her mouth.

Kat choked and swallowed. "About what?" she asked thickly.

"He was leaving us alone."

"Why?"

"So we could talk." He shrugged. "Get to know each other." He watched her sip at the tea. "Maybe so you could tell me I'm delicious and sexy. Again."

Kat set her mug down with a thump. "Again?" She repeated the word cautiously, handling it as if it had sharp and dangerous edges.

"Again."

Giving a resigned sigh, she gazed at his expressionless face. Only the amused gleam in his eyes gave him away. He was just too bland, too cute for words she decided with disgust. And far too pleased with himself. "Don't worry," she said calmly, masking her annoyance. "I seem to mumble a lot of nonsense when I'm asleep, but I rarely act on it." She pointedly changed the subject. "But as long as we have some time, there are a couple of things I'd like to discuss."

"Fire away. If it's personal, I figure we have about two minutes before Claude comes back. He's too nosy to stay away for long."

"Aren't there any helicopters around here to pick up people who are stranded?" she demanded, getting right to the point.

"Sure. In emergencies. But you've found a place to roost, so they won't want to be bothered."

"How much snow is out there?"

"Almost a foot. May be more by the end of the day. It's

too much to dig out that low-slung car of yours and get it back on the road.''

"That's a fact," Claude said, swinging back through the door. "You'll be here for several days. Count on it."

"I thought you were dusting." Mac didn't look away from Kat's expressive face. She was troubled, and he had a hunch that it wasn't just the sparks between them that were bothering her.

"Yeah, well, things weren't as bad as I thought," Claude snapped. "Why are you so hell-bent to get out of here, Kat? You know you're as welcome as the spring thaws. You can stay here as long as you like. It ain't Davy, is it? I thought you two got on like a house afire."

Talk about barging in where angels fear to tread, Mac thought. Claude was good at that, and he'd probably get more out of their unexpected guest than anyone—except maybe Davy. Mac leaned back, studying Kat's shocked expression.

"Davy?" she sputtered. "There's nothing wrong with Davy. He's, he's—"

"Delicious?" prompted Mac.

Slanting him a narrowed glance, she nodded. "Among other things." Turning back to Claude, she said fiercely, "I hope you never say anything like that when he's around. He's a wonderful little guy and he'd be very hurt."

Claude snorted. "Hell, I know that. The only reason I asked was because I knew he was reading in the office. So, what's the rush?"

"I have a job to do," Kat told him, exasperated at his persistence.

"I thought you were on vacation."

Mac sat quietly, watching Kat. Claude was doing just fine, he reflected. Just fine.

"I am. I just wasn't quite—"

"Honest?" Mac asked blandly.

"Open," she corrected, sending him a hard look. "The whole thing's just a little complicated, and I saw no sense in getting into it if I was going to be taking right off."

"Well, it looks like we're gonna have nothing but time on our hands, so why don't you tell us about it." Claude pulled up a chair and joined them. "Maybe we can help. We're good at that, ain't we, Mac?" He gave Mac's foot a warning nudge and glared at him.

"Oh, yeah," Mac said dryly. "We're great."

"See?" Claude grinned encouragingly at her. "Tell us about it."

"It's a dull story," she warned. "You'll probably be bored silly." She looked from one to the other and gave up when they just gazed expectantly at her. "I'm an environmental chemist, working out of—"

"Denver," Claude interjected. "You told us that. Are you one of them tree huggers?"

Kat shrugged. "Sometimes. Most of the time I'm holed up in a lab trying to figure out how to clear the air or enrich the soil."

Mac listened quietly, drawing his own conclusions. If her expression was any indication, she was dedicated, an idealist who would work herself into the ground for the right cause. Any way you looked at it, it was a hell of a combination. And exactly what he didn't need on the ranch.

"Right now we're working on animal anomalies," she continued quietly.

"Say what?" Claude raised his brows questioningly.

"An animal that differs from the norm. It may be abnormal or just peculiar. It could be a two-headed cow or a three-legged cat or an albino horse. You've surely run into things like that on the ranch. Well, if the changes are persistent, we investigate them."

"So what brings you here?"

Neither man looked bored, she reflected. Claude was curious, and Mac was...what? His steady gaze didn't leave her face, but she had a feeling that something had changed in the last few seconds—and that the change wasn't necessarily good.

"We've heard of a colony of scentless skunks in the area. In fact, we've had several reports over the last five years, so that means they're breeding and it's not just a fluke. I'm here to check them out. *Then* I go on vacation."

Mac finally joined the conversation. "What happened to John Price?"

"Our field technician?" she asked with a blink. "You know John?"

"We've corresponded. The skunks," he added in a gentle voice that made her wince, "are on the property I lease, so he asked permission to conduct the experiments."

"And you gave it," she said encouragingly.

"I gave it. To him. What happened to him?" he repeated.

"He has the mumps. Both of his kids are down with them. He just called and told me about it yesterday. That's why I got off to a late start. I had to collect his paperwork."

"Why?"

She stared at Mac, puzzled. "Why what?"

"Why you, for starters."

"There was no one else," she said, giving a slight shrug. "He was going to give the information he collected to me, so I was the obvious one."

"The obvious one to what?"

"Aren't you listening?" Exasperation tinged her voice. "The one to come here."

"And do what?"

She heaved a sigh. "Replace John. Do what he was going to do."

"Like hell you will."

Three

"**L**ike hell I *won't.*" Kat stiffened, her narrowed eyes blazing blue fire.

"Now, folks, let's calm down here. Shoutin' ain't gonna get us anywhere." Claude's pacifying tone did not have a noticeably soothing effect on either of them.

"I'm *not* shouting."

"Butt out, Claude."

"Reckon I'll go finish dusting." Claude scooted his chair back and got up. "Now, Kat, I don't know what you're like when you get riled, but he can argue the hind leg off a donkey. You two make your peace before Davy comes in and finds you squabblin'." The door swished as he went through it again.

With an effort that was almost visible, Kat reined in her temper. This was no time to go off half-cocked, she reminded herself. There was simply too much at stake. Calm. She would remain calm, even though he was obstinate enough to drive a saint crazy.

"I don't see the problem here," she said peaceably. "I'm sure we can come up with a reasonable solution."

Mac popped a piece of coffee cake in his mouth and eyed her grimly. "Which means that you want to talk until you change my mind. Well, go ahead. Try."

"I said reasonable," Kat said through clenched teeth. "That usually involves a discussion, not one person inciting another. For heaven's sake, what's the problem here?"

"You," he said bluntly. "You're the problem. You're a city girl, wearing city clothes, and you don't know diddly squat about this part of the country. Probably don't know anything about skunks, either."

Kat brightened. "Hah, you're wrong there." She mentally summoned up the information she'd read while eating lunch at her desk yesterday. "They're nocturnal. During the winter, they burrow into tunnels or other dark, warm places. Although they chiefly hunt at night, at this time of the year they instinctively begin to get ready for the coming food shortage by almost continuous feeding, even during the day. They convert their food supply into body fat that will carry them through the winter."

"That's textbook stuff. I mean *really* know about skunks."

Figuring she was on a roll, Kat ignored his comment. "After this stupid snow thaws, I estimate I'll have about three weeks or so before your real winter begins. During that time, I'll find them and get the blood samples I need," she ended triumphantly.

Momentarily diverted, he asked with genuine interest, "How are you going to get blood from a skunk?"

"With a dart gun and a syringe." Her matter-of-fact tone concealed her own reservations. It couldn't be terribly complicated, she assured herself. You find the critter, use the little dart gun to put it to sleep for a few minutes, collect the blood, tag the skunk's ear, spray a dab of paint somewhere on it, make sure the critter wakes up, then go find another one and repeat the process.

It was simple, at least it was according to the gospel of John, who had given her precise instructions over the telephone. But then, she remembered with sudden doubt, John had been doing things like this for over twenty years. She, on the other hand, had never handled a gun. Not even a cap pistol as a kid.

Mac shook his head in disgust. "Assuming there are such things as scentless skunks, how are you going to tell them from the ones that smell like pure poison?"

"Believe me, not by standing around and letting them take aim at me. My job right now is to get blood samples— of every skunk I can find. Later, we'll run DNA tests. If any of the results are markedly different, John will have the pleasant job of coming back and flushing out the ones we'll want to examine. I don't know and I don't really care how he'll do it."

"And where are you going to stay while you're doing all this?"

"Wherever John was going to stay. His file is in my car, and I haven't had a chance to read his itinerary. But I'm sure his motel won't quibble about which one of us uses the room."

"Have you ever done any camping?"

Kat blinked. Camping? Shrugging, she decided that following Mac in a conversation was as tricky as tracking down a pollution source. Finally she shook her head, opting for honesty. "Only in my own backyard as a kid. With a friend. We had flashlights, a huge midnight snack and an open back door. We…"

Her voice faded and she stared at him. "Are you telling me that he was going to *camp*?"

Mac's nod was grim. "Yeah. No motels, no hot water,

no bathtub, no bathroom, period. Nature in the raw. Visits from deer and an occasional grizzly.''

It was the underlying satisfaction in his voice that did it. That and his certainty that she was in over her head. Horrified, she heard herself say, ''Then I guess I'll just have to rent some camping equipment.''

''The...hell...you...will.''

They were right back where they had started, Kat thought glumly. Probably even further, because this time he wasn't merely surprised. He was furious.

''Mac, be reasonable,'' she began. Her words were cut off by his bleak expression.

''Reasonable?'' He got up with a muttered oath and walked over to the sink. Bracing his hands on the counter, he stared out the window at the falling snow. ''How reasonable would it be for me to let a woman who's a complete greenhorn go out in the wilderness alone? To face the chance of dying of exposure?''

''The way your wife did?'' she asked softly. When he turned around to face her, leaning against the counter, arms crossed on his chest, she said, ''Claude told me.''

Mac nodded. ''Yeah,'' he said evenly, ''exactly the way she did. So forget it, sweetheart. I've got enough on my conscience.''

''I can understand—''

''No, you can't. Unless you've been responsible for someone dying, you don't have a clue.''

''I'm simply trying to say—''

''Well, don't. Try listening, instead. Forget the skunk. Forget your job. Go to Yellowstone and play tourist. Take pictures of the geysers. Do anything you damn well please—except play the intrepid scientist on my property.''

''All right.'' Kat held up her hands in a peaceable gesture. ''I won't camp out.''

''You bet your sweet butt you won't.''

"I'll find a place to stay."

"Where?"

She heaved an exasperated sigh. "How should I know? Trust me, I'll find a place. I'll drive over every day, find the skunks, do what I have to do and take off long before dark. Surely you can't object to that."

"I can't?" His voice was grim. "A storm's a storm whether it sweeps in during the day or night."

"Dammit, Mac, I'm sorry about what happened, sorry you and Davy were left alone, but I'm not your wife. I'm not going to die out there."

"Damn straight you won't, because you're not going to set foot in the area."

She took a fortifying breath. It was obvious that Mac was in the habit of giving orders. Well, in Denver, so was she. It was just as obvious that his commands were normally followed—without arguments. So were hers. Actually, she reflected, if she had a choice, she'd like nothing better than to follow his advice—to forget the whole miserable idea and trot off to Yellowstone. The last thing in the world she wanted to do was head for a place where the only thing between her and a grizzly was a flimsy piece of canvas.

But she didn't have a choice. This could be a vital step in their research on adaptation. "Mac," she said calmly, "I have a letter from you in the car, giving permission for someone from our lab to be there."

"Giving John Price permission." His voice was cool. "And before I did, I checked his credentials. He's been doing fieldwork all around the world for the last twenty years. He can take care of himself. You, on the other hand, have been cloistered in a lab."

He had a point, Kat admitted reluctantly. A good one. What she knew about surviving in the wilderness could be expressed in five letters. Zippo. Her limited fieldwork ex-

perience had taken place almost ten years ago and had been
closely supervised. None of it had required coping with the
great outdoors for an extended period of time, and nothing
she'd learned since would be of any help.

Not only was the idea of acquiring all the necessary
equipment mind-boggling, the prospect of managing on her
own was downright scary. She didn't have the foggiest idea
how to handle even the basics—like setting up a tent or
cooking over an open stove. Food always seemed to be a
problem, she reflected glumly. She wasn't terrific with it
anywhere—even at home with an electric range and a
microwave.

"What if I hire a guide?" she asked suddenly, giving
Mac a hopeful glance. "Surely there must be someone
around here who takes people backpacking and camping."
The idea seemed better with each passing second, especially if that someone could cook. "It's the perfect solution," she said with quick enthusiasm. "He could take care
of all the stuff you're worried about and ride shotgun while
I work. The lab will cover the costs, we'll help boost the
local economy and I'll get the samples I need before winter
comes charging in. What do you think?"

What did he think? That she was going to drive him right
around the bend. In the first place, the whole scheme was
crazy. Scentless skunks. Only someone from the city could
have come up with such a weird idea. And if he let her run
around on her own, he'd never have a minute's peace.

Okay, he admitted wearily, maybe he wasn't entirely rational on the subject. History probably wouldn't repeat itself. Kat might be safe—but considering her lack of experience, he couldn't count on it. Dammit, he *wouldn't*
count on it. Once in a lifetime was enough for any man.
He wasn't going to tempt fate.

As for a guide, sure there were some in the area. He
knew most of them were decent, hardworking men. And

there wasn't a single one that he'd trust alone in close quarters with Kat for two or three weeks.

Aside from that, he admitted ruefully, there was a basic disturbance factor. Just knowing she was around would keep his hormones in an uproar. He wouldn't get a damn thing done and his temper would be sour enough to curdle milk.

"Well?" Kat tapped her foot impatiently. "What do you think about a guide?"

She wasn't going to give up, he thought grimly. She was as stubborn as he was. The only difference was that arguing seemed to energize her, and he was already worn out. A night without sleep wasn't helping. Pushing away from the sink, he said, "I think we'll talk about it later. Right now, I have to get out to the barn."

"But—"

"Later, Kat."

Frustrated, she watched him shrug into his shearling coat and push open the door to the enclosed back porch. She regained her voice just as it slammed behind him. "Mac Ryder, you are without a doubt the most—"

"Mule-stubborn man in Wyoming," Claude finished for her. His gaze was sympathetic when she spun around to face him. "Yep, he's bullheaded, all right. Won't give an inch once he makes up his mind. 'Course, sometimes it's good. He's kept the ranch going and he's making money on it because he's too ornery to ever quit." He snorted and reached for the handle of the refrigerator. "On the other hand, sometimes it's bad. Right or wrong, once he puts his foot down, it stays planted." His muffled voice came from within the refrigerator. "A man can miss a heap of good that way."

She made an exasperated sound. "What's so important out there in the barn that he has to go right now?"

Claude emerged with his hands full. "My guess

is...nothing. I figure he needs time to think, maybe shore up his arguments a little.''

Kat shot him a speculative glance. ''You mean he hasn't totally made up his mind?''

''Well, I wouldn't give up too easy, if I was you. What I heard was more of a testing-the-waters, arguing kind of no. If he'd meant it for sure, he wouldn't have walked away saying he'd talk about it later.''

''Then I've still got a chance.''

''If you think fast. Latest word is that the cold front is passing and it's going to warm up real fast. Don't be surprised if you wake up in the morning and find the sun shining.''

''Tomorrow?'' Kat groaned. ''I thought the weather man said we'd have this snow for two or three days. I need more time to work on him.''

Claude shrugged. ''Even with all their fancy gadgets, they get fooled. Think of it this way—if you do manage to stay, the less snow on the ground, the better it is for you. The faster it melts, the sooner you can go skunk hunting.''

''Yeah. And the sooner I can get my clothes out of the car.''

''You look just fine to me.''

''Claude, look at me,'' she invited with a sweep of her hand. ''I appreciate the loan, but your jeans fit me like a second skin.''

He gave her an appreciative grin. ''Like I said, you look just fine to me.''

''Men.'' She dropped in a chair by the table and scowled at him.

The disgusted mutter drew another grin from him. ''My wife used to sound just like that when she was ready to throw a skillet at me.''

''You were married?''

"Yep." He turned to the stove. "For a long time. She died a few years back."

"I'm sorry, Claude."

"Me, too."

Bringing the subject back to a less painful topic, she asked, "Is anyone else out there with Mac?"

"Doubt it." Claude shrugged. "As I said, there's really not much to do. I think he's out there taking a breather."

"Well, he's not going to get it." She jumped to her feet. "Claude, do you have a jacket and some boots I can borrow?"

"You goin' after him?"

"You bet I am. The last thing I need is for him to come up with a good argument out there." She grinned. "He needs to understand that it's to his advantage to help me."

Claude cocked a brow. "How's that?"

"The sooner I get my job done, the sooner he'll have me out of his hair."

"Lord save me from a determined woman," he muttered piously.

"You got that right. What about the boots and jacket?"

Mac paced the length of the cold barn, keeping his hands stuffed in his pockets for warmth. It was dark, but he didn't bother with the lights. He knew every square inch of the building and could have walked through it blindfolded.

Drawn by the sound of his footsteps, the curious horses poked their heads out over the edges of the stalls. He absently rubbed noses and scratched between ears as he worked his way down the wide walkway.

But he couldn't move fast enough to escape the image of Kat's shimmering blue eyes, their color deepening as her emotions moved from outright pleading to gathering wrath. She didn't give up easily. Hell, she didn't give up at all.

She was probably sitting in the kitchen with Claude, working on the next round of arguments.

If her intensity was any indication, this skunk project of hers ranked right up there with global peace and world famine. And he still didn't know why. Of course, he could have asked her, but he hadn't—and he didn't intend to. If he showed any interest at all, she'd just start all over again.

The odds were already against him. Kat wanted to stay, Davy wanted her to stay and Claude felt the same way. Hell, *he* even wanted her to stay, Mac reflected as he perched on a bale of hay.

He liked having a woman in the house. Liked having Kat in the house, he amended silently. Liked the way she smelled like wildflowers even though she was using his soap and shampoo. Liked the way she unconsciously shifted pillows on the couch and moved things, adding feminine touches that he hadn't even known he'd missed.

He liked seeing the way she filled out Claude's jeans, the way she had clung to him when he'd carried her to bed last night and the way she laughed when she was with Davy. They were images that would haunt him for weeks to come.

But he had been through this once. He'd met and married a city girl, promised to protect her as well as love and cherish her. And he'd failed her. She had died because of his negligence. She had gone out riding one fair afternoon, was caught in a sudden storm and died of exposure—leaving behind a baby who would never know his mother and a husband unable to forgive himself.

No, by God, he wouldn't do it again. It didn't matter how much he wanted to taste Kat, to feel her silky skin beneath his, to have her wrapped around him, her body brushing against his in a rhythm as old as Eden. He had survived once; he wasn't so sure he could do it again.

The barn door flew open and slammed shut with a shudder that alarmed the horses. He murmured soothingly to a startled bay, turning his head when someone moved across the dirt floor.

"Mac?" Kat's uncertain voice drifted down to him. "Are you there?"

"Yeah."

"Good grief, it's spooky in here. Ouch! Dammit. What was that?"

He heard the thump and shook his head. "The corner of a stall."

"Why don't you turn on some lights?"

"I don't need them, city girl. I know where everything is."

"Well, I don't." She sounded breathless.

"Stand still. I'll come and get you." As he neared her, he reached out and flipped a switch, watching Kat blink in the sudden surge of light. His hands dropped on her shoulders and he swung her around to face him, giving rein to the sudden anger licking through him. "What the hell do you mean coming out here in this weather? It was idiotic. Anything could have happened to you."

Kat grinned at him. "Not a chance. Claude bundled me up until I looked like a sausage, then he wouldn't let me off the porch until he checked the path. Your footprints were nice and clear so he figured even I couldn't get lost between here and the house. It's, uh, only fifty yards...or so."

Her voice dwindled away, fading to a whisper. The smile left her face and her slim fingers touched his cheek. "Mac, don't look so fierce. I'm fine. I'm sorry. I didn't mean to worry you."

He skimmed his hands over the scarf covering her hair and wondered if she had any idea how much he wanted her.

Stunned by the need in his narrowed eyes, Kat caught her breath.

"Mac?"

"Yeah?"

They both whispered, as if their voices would shatter something precious.

"If we don't move, something's going to happen."

"Count on it."

"You want me, don't you?"

His fingers tightened in her hair. "In every way."

Kat cleared her throat. "Maybe we can write this off as academic curiosity, but why aren't you doing something about it?"

"Because of a damned inconvenient sense of honor," he said with a sharp sigh. He tilted her face until he could see her eyes. They were alive with feminine curiosity and trust. It was the trust that did him in.

He backed her up to the bale of hay and nudged her to sit on it. Propping a booted foot next to her hip, he rested a forearm on his thigh and leaned over her.

"I ache with wanting you," he said bluntly. "I didn't get an hour's sleep last night because of it. And if you stay around here for very long, you'll end up in my bed."

Kat blinked up at him, her eyes wary. "You make that sound as if I wouldn't have a vote."

"Oh, you'd vote," he assured her. "I'm talking about seduction, not rape."

"Then what's the problem?" She scooted back to lean against the wall.

"The *problem*," he said, gently emphasizing the word, "is that I'm not in the market for marriage or any permanent commitment. If it happens, what we'll have is great sex. When it's over, it's over. You'll go back to the city, and I'll stay right here where I belong."

"With Davy, Claude and your horses," she said thoughtfully.

"Right."

"Sounds like it could get lonely."

"It can and it does, but I'd rather deal with that than guilt and regret."

With an effort Kat kept her voice as cool as his. "You seem to be making an assumption that any woman who comes near you—"

"Not any woman. You."

"All right, that *I* am looking for marriage and commitment."

"And you're not?"

She shook her head. "It's the last thing on my mind," she said honestly. "I wouldn't leave my job for anything. I have a condo on the outskirts of Denver, my family and friends are all within driving distance, and I can't imagine changing anything in my life."

"So what are you saying?" Mac's brows rose inquiringly. "Are you open to having an affair? With me?"

"Oh, for Pete's sake, you have a one-track mind, Ryder." Kat gave him a scathing glance. "No, that's not what I'm saying. What I'm trying to get through that block of wood you call a head is that I'm twenty-nine. I've been making my own decisions for a long time now. And, frankly, very few of those decisions have revolved around a man's bed."

She gave him another scowl for good measure. "Just because you think we'll end up in bed doesn't mean it's going to happen. In fact, I can almost guarantee you that it won't."

His sudden grin startled her, and she eyed him with deep wariness. "What? What's that look for?"

"Are you a gambler?" He dropped down beside her and waited.

Kat groaned. "Can't you stick to the point for more than two seconds?"

"Same point, different angle." He nudged her with his elbow. "So, are you a gambler?"

"I occasionally take a flyer on a long shot," she admitted. "But I prefer to have the odds in my favor."

"Okay, what do you think of these odds? I'll help you find your damn skunks."

"*What?*"

Mac held up his hand to stop her. "I'll even help you get the blood samples."

She eyed him with deep suspicion. "And?"

"And for the time we're together, we let nature take its course," he said with a shrug. "I'm going to do my damnedest to seduce you, to get you in my bed."

"And if you don't?" she asked cautiously.

He studied her wary expression with narrowed eyes. "Then I have a feeling that we'll both be losing. You'll get your samples and be free to go with a clear conscience. But I'm betting we end up as lovers. If we do, it's all over when you leave. With no regrets."

"Done," she said promptly, holding out her hand to seal the bargain.

He took it and held on to it, tugging her closer. "Do you always jump in with both feet like this?" he asked with deep interest.

A smile drew up one corner of her mouth. "Nope. But in this case, I have an ace in the hole."

"What's that?" He tipped back his hat, giving her a good view of the gleam in his eyes. "Or can you tell me?"

"Sure," she said blithely. "I just happen to know myself, and basically I'm not a passionate or a sensual person."

"You're not—" Mac coughed and came to a dead stop, looking astounded. Wondering if she remembered her response to the kiss at her bedroom door, he asked, "What the devil gave you that idea?"

She shrugged. "I've always known. It's no big deal. Mother Nature has a way of compensating, you know."

Mac shook his head, as much to clear it as in response to her statement. "I never thought about it."

"It's true." Kat leaned her head comfortably on his shoulder. "I got an extra dab of intelligence. I'm quite bright, you know."

"Do tell." Mac looked down at her tumbled hair and grinned.

"Yep. I'm a certified genius," she said complacently. "Ran right off the charts when they tested me. I can't take any credit for it, though. It runs in my genes. My whole family is smart."

Draping an arm around her shoulder, he tugged her closer, his smile broadening when she snuggled against him. "So what are you doing out in the middle of nowhere chasing skunks, if you're so smart?"

"That's only because poor John got the mumps," she said, chuckling. "Normally I'm in a lab coat, in my own private section of the lab, doing brilliant things." She looked up at him. "Quit laughing. It's all true. But I haven't quite figured out why you changed your mind. One minute you were ready to kick me off the place as soon as it quit snowing, and the next you offered to play guide."

"And lover," he reminded her.

"That remains to be seen." She nudged him with her shoulder. "So, why the switch?"

"Several reasons. I *did* give permission for someone to come and check out the situation."

"And your word is your bond."

"Something like that. And I had already figured out that you were going to keep arguing about it until one of us gave in, so I wasn't too surprised when you followed me out here. If I said yes, I knew I wouldn't get any work done around here while I was worrying about you. I also knew I wouldn't keep my hands off you if we were together for any length of time, so I finally decided that laying my cards on the table would solve most of the problems. Satisfied?''

"Yeah. It makes a weird kind of sense.'' She pulled away from him and got to her feet. ''After all that, I really hate to burst your bubble, but I didn't come out here to plead my cause.''

"No?''

Smiling at his skeptical expression, she shook her head. ''No. I thought about it but decided I'd try later—maybe after dinner, when you were well fed and your resistance was down. What I really wanted to do was talk to you about Davy.''

Four

——

"**D**o you have a few minutes?"

Kat stood in the doorway of the office, hands on her hips, looking at Mac. He was studying an IRS form with a total lack of enthusiasm.

"I can't believe I've finally caught up with you. Do you realize it's been two days since I asked if we could talk?" she asked in mild exasperation. "If I'd known how hard you'd be to corner I wouldn't have left the barn until I'd had my say." Glancing at her watch, she groaned. "Davy will be home from school in a few minutes and then we're leaving to get the supplies."

Right on the heels of her announcement in the barn, Mac had bundled her back into the house, saying it was too cold to stay outside. Davy had joined them when they'd entered the house, and since she hadn't wanted to bring the matter up in front of him, she had held her peace.

Sunlight awoke her the next morning, just as Claude had

predicted. Mac left early to spend the day with his men, arranging work schedules for the next few weeks, while she played games with Davy and watched the amazing transformation wrought by the thaw. Clumps of snow fell from trees, displaying the still-green leaves of a huge cottonwood and the glistening needles of the pines. The pristine ground cover gradually revealed sections of a grassy yard surrounded by graveled roads.

"It's about Davy," she told him. "And I'd rather not have this discussion in front of him."

Mac leaned back in the swivel chair, enjoying her look of simmering impatience. For a woman who claimed she wasn't passionate, she sure had a lot of emotions bubbling beneath the surface, he reflected, shoving a stack of papers aside. He was surprised she hadn't cornered him before this if it was so urgent. As far as Kat was concerned, patience apparently wasn't a virtue. It was simply another word for being forced to wait.

He gestured for her to join him. "How fast can you talk? I've been tying up some loose ends, and I figured we'd have plenty of time for conversation once we left for town. I guess I was wrong." He waved her to a chair. "Okay, what's on your mind?"

Kat rounded the desk, heading for the chair next to him. Now that she had his full attention, she realized she didn't quite know how to begin. She should have practiced a nice, tactful approach, she thought uneasily, tucking one foot beneath her as she sat beside him. Some people required a gradual introduction to any subject more complex than the weather, and she didn't know Mac well enough to gauge his preference. All she knew for certain was that she didn't want to blow the whole thing.

Mac waited. Doubt and anxiety flickered on her expressive face. "Okay, Kat, you've got the floor," he finally said. "Are you going to use it?"

When her blue eyes flashed in irritation, Mac's enjoyment deepened. Kat would no doubt consider it a serious character defect on his part, he reflected, but he couldn't resist the urge to provoke her. His inclination had always run toward fractious females, and she was as troublesome as they came, even though she was trying to be the perfect guest. He found her attempts to control her exasperation fascinating—and sexy as hell.

"Okay." She lifted her shoulders in a slight shrug. "Do you prefer to have news thrown at you, or do you like a gradual progression of information?"

He grinned. "If the place is on fire, I'd like to know up front. Other than that, it doesn't matter."

"Fine." She eased back in the chair. "Remember the other night when I told you I was, uh, fairly bright?"

He nodded. "The way I heard it was that you were a genius."

"Did you believe me?"

"Sure." He shrugged. "Why would you lie about it?"

"I wouldn't. Did I also tell you that my parents fall into the same category, as do my grandparents on my mother's side, my brother and my nephew."

"Great. I'm happy for you. Is this leading somewhere?" he asked politely.

"Give me a minute here, will you?" Kat frowned at him. "The point is, that when you're in that narrow academic percentile, you eventually tend to be placed in special classes or schools where you mingle with others who are much the same."

"Kat—"

"And soon you begin to recognize the signs when you meet others—"

"*Kat*. Pretend the house is on fire," he said wearily.

"All right." She lifted her shoulders in a slight shrug. "Davy is one."

Mac stared at her. "Is one what?"

"A genius," she said, not bothering to hide her exasperation. "Isn't that what we're talking about?"

"After all your tap dancing, I'm not sure."

"Well we were, and he is."

He gave an exasperated sigh of his own, ignoring her incredible statement. "If you're so damn smart, how come you can't manage a simple, straightforward conversation? Do you have to talk in circles?"

"I learned very early in the game that people don't relate to eggheads." She grinned. "So I was smart enough to avoid sounding like one. Now, while I admit I make a fascinating diversion, do you want to discuss me or your precocious son?"

"Let's talk about Davy," he said definitely. "Sure, he's a smart kid, but I've never had the impression that he was a little Einstein." He propped his feet on the corner of the desk and gazed thoughtfully at the pointed toes of his boots. He finally looked up and shot her a level glance. "What makes you think so?"

Kat shook her head. "Oh, ye of little faith. I told you. After a while, the brainy ones are easy to recognize."

"How sure are you?"

Her hesitation was so slight he almost missed it. "Until he's tested, nothing is really certain, but every instinct is telling me it's true. And if it is, you need to do something right away—before he becomes a very frustrated little boy."

Mac's eyes narrowed. "What do you mean?"

"Well, for starters, look at the way he talks. He certainly doesn't sound like your normal six-year-old. And he's already playing games with adults, trying to adapt to their expectations." She held up her hand to stop him from interrupting. "No, wait a minute. Let me finish. You and Claude are vitally important to him, and he wants to please you. Believe me, he's got you guys pegged. He knows you think he's a sharp little boy, so that's what he shows you. No more, no less.''

''I don't believe it.'' Mac tapped a pencil on the edge of the desk. ''He wouldn't lie to us.''

''You're right, he wouldn't. I think it's instinctive rather than deliberate. I doubt if he even realizes what he's doing, but the end result is he's making you happy and getting the approval he needs.''

She prodded his arm with a slim finger for emphasis. ''I did it all the time when I was a kid. Not with my family— I didn't have to play games with them. I did it with the kids in school. When I was in a regular school, I mean. I wanted them to like me, and I knew they wouldn't if I came off as a big brain. If I had shown what I was capable of in class, I wouldn't have had a single friend.''

''That's not proof.''

Kat sighed. She knew from experience that this wasn't an easy thing to accept. ''You want proof? Let's talk about his reading material for a minute.'' She waved at the shelf of books placed low for Davy's convenience.

Mac scowled at her. ''What's the matter with it? I admit some of the books are a grade or two above his level, but that's so he can stretch a bit.''

''Oh, Mac.'' She reached out and covered his hand with hers, her soft voice urgent. ''I know this is a shock, but don't kill the messenger, okay? I'm trying to help you— and Davy, of course. You've done a wonderful job with him. But if what I suspect is true—and I absolutely believe it is—you need to *know*. Now. And you need to make some plans for him.''

''Okay, I'll bite. What's wrong with his reading mate- rial?'' Mac turned his hand and laced his fingers through hers, holding her captive. ''Isn't it politically correct for these days?''

"I'm not talking about anything as stupid as that," she said, frowning. "I'm talking about his ability. Do you know what he reads when he comes down here after you've gone to bed?"

The expression in Mac's eyes was impossible to read, but she felt his sudden tension. "Don't look so worried," she said lightly. "He reads your books." She stopped, blinking with thought. "I hope you don't have a stash of porno stuff hidden away."

"My books?" Mac couldn't have been more astounded if she told him his horses were square dancing in the barn.

"Yours. I asked him to read me a story the other night and he climbed up on a chair and pulled down that thriller." She pointed to the book on the coffee table. "And he read it—word perfect. Earlier, I played blackjack with him, and the kid counts cards like a pro, which means his math skills could be extraordinary. So don't be too smug about getting him into bed by playing strip poker." She chuckled at his startled expression.

"He told you about that?"

"Yeah. He even tried to con me into a game." She disposed of the incident with an airy wave of her hand. "But that's beside the point. One last thing—he probably has a photographic memory. I gave him the rule book for chess and after he read it, he almost beat me. And, Mac," she added with a wry grin, "I'm a master player."

His fingers tightened around hers. "Anything else?

"That's the extent of my so-called proof, but you need to think about his school. Mac, he must be bored silly. He's too nice a kid to deliberately aggravate anyone, but practically the first thing he said to me was that his teacher thinks he's more trouble than a handful of hornets."

"Yeah, I know," he sighed. "She told me he lacks discipline in the classroom."

"Bullfeathers. He's just finishing his work in the first

few minutes, and then he has nothing to do except find something else to occupy his mind."

"How can you be so sure?"

Kat grinned. "I asked him, and he told me."

"Dammit, he's my son. Why didn't he tell *me*."

"Because you didn't ask," she said simply. When he got to his feet and paced the length of the room, she sat quietly. The taut set of his shoulders spoke volumes about his anger—all self-directed, if she was any judge.

In the short time she had known Mac, one thing had come across loud and clear—he had a protective instinct as large as his ranch. He was responsible for the small, the young, the old and the weak, which meant just about everyone in the world. He wouldn't easily forgive himself for missing something like this.

"Mac." Her voice was gentle. "Davy's a bright little boy, and he's found a solution for his problem. He simply doesn't talk about it. Of course it's only a temporary answer, but he doesn't know that.

"On the other hand, he won't lie if you ask him a direct question. I've got a nine-year-old nephew who's taught me everything I know about quizzing kids. Then, of course, I had my own experience to fall back on. But I had one advantage that Davy doesn't have. My parents were more or less expecting the family trait to show up in me, so they were looking for signs."

He turned to face her, his dark eyes bleak. "I should have known."

"How? Are you a mind reader? You've got yourself a wonderful, well-adjusted little boy. He's not much of a talker or complainer, and he wants the people he loves to be happy. You wouldn't be happy if he told you he was troubled about school."

He looked at her in disbelief. "I don't need protecting. For God's sake, I'm the adult here."

"I know that as well as you, but Davy doesn't. And—here's the important part—he doesn't understand what it is about him that's different. He knows there's something, but he doesn't know what it is, so how can he sit down and initiate a father-son conversation about it?"

"He seems to do well enough with you." His tone was sharper than he'd intended.

Kat jumped to her feet, bristling. "You're right. He talks with me, and you'd better be damned glad that he does. This way, you're getting a little warning."

Folding her arms across her chest, she demanded, "Are you going to complain because I discovered this, or are you going to get your butt in gear and do something about it? He's already having problems in the first grade. How unhappy will he be in another year or two?"

Turning away, she walked over to the window and gazed out over the backyard, watching the activity down by the barn. The ranch hands were loading hay into a truck as Claude looked on.

She didn't hear him move, but one second Mac was on the other side of the room and the next, his hands were at her waist, pulling her back against him. His arms wrapped around her, and his lips touched her hair. "Just give me a minute to get used to the idea, okay?"

Kat felt his turmoil and slowly relaxed against him, offering what comfort she could. She felt his solid strength against every inch of her body and nestled closer. There was a lingering fragrance of soap from his morning shower, heat and a faint overriding of dust and sweat. Most of all, there was an essence of clean male that was uniquely Mac. It was a potent combination. A part of her mind that wasn't lulled by the contact, reminded her that nice as it was, this was not a good idea. Mac's body was already indicating that it wanted more than comfort.

"Okay, tiger." He gave her a final squeeze and released her. "What do you suggest?"

Now that he was willing to move ahead, she hesitated one last time. What she was going to propose would cost money. Perhaps quite a bit. "Testing and a computer, for starters," she finally said. "I know some very good people in Denver who could do the testing, and I could select a computer system and software for him. I set up Cody, my nephew, with one, so I'm an old hand at something like this."

She met his gaze and saw that he was waiting, so she said baldly, "I suppose there's a delicate way to say this, but it will be fairly expensive."

Mac shrugged away the implied concern. "Ten years ago that might have been a problem. It isn't now."

Kat brightened. "Good. This place where we're going for supplies, is it a decent-sized town? Does it have a good bookstore and computer center?"

"Not the one I had planned on going to. We'll just go the opposite direction and drive a little longer. No problem." He leaned back against the desk, his thumbs tucked in his front pockets. "How long will it take you to set the computer up?"

"Are we still going skunk hunting the day after tomorrow?"

He nodded.

"There'll be plenty of time. I'll get the computer working when we get back from shopping. Davy and I will play with it tonight and tomorrow after school. He'll catch on fast."

"Okay. When we get to town, I'll get the stuff for our trip while you two hit the computer store."

"And a good bookstore," she reminded him.

"And a bookstore," he agreed.

She reached for a pen and notepad and began making a

list. Looking up a moment later, she asked, "Do I have a budget?"

"Get what you think he'll need."

"Good." She grinned. "I love spending other people's money."

"Kat?"

"Mmm?" She didn't look up.

"Thank you."

An hour later the three of them piled into Mac's blue pickup and headed for town. Davy, sitting by the window, chattered excitedly about the computer. "Will it have games?"

"Yep." Kat, tucked between the two Ryders, slid her arm around Davy's shoulder and gave him a hug. "But I'll warn you right now, I don't approve of the violent ones. You'll get plenty of excitement, though." Turning to face Mac, she said softly, "And he'll learn a lot."

Mac reached over for her hand and placed it on his thigh, holding it firmly in place with his larger one. "I have a feeling we're all going to do some learning in the next few weeks."

Davy turned a worried face to Mac. "Whose computer will it be?"

"Well," Mac said, casting a quick glance at him, "I guess it will belong to the family, but you'll probably be the only one using it for a while."

"Will I have to ask each time I want to use it?"

Kat sat silently, one hand on Mac's thigh, the other on Davy's shoulder, feeling the tension in both of them. She pressed against Mac and gave his son an encouraging squeeze.

Mac's fingers tightened around hers. "We'll have to talk about it and set up some guidelines."

"Like we did for the TV?"

Mac pushed back his hat a notch. "Yeah, something like that. I don't want you sitting in front of it all day."

"But you won't get mad when I touch it?" Davy persevered.

Mac took his eyes off the road and glanced at his son. Davy seemed to be holding his breath and his eyes were dark with worry. Mac bit back the impatient comment he was about to make and bought some time by turning on the main highway. Finally he said in a neutral tone, "Do I get mad when you turn on the TV?" He felt Kat relax against him and knew he'd hit the right note.

Davy shook his head. "No."

"Then why would I act any different with a computer?"

"I don't know." His shrug indicated that adult behavior was beyond his understanding. "Mr. Bloom got mad when I touched the one in the office, and I thought maybe kids weren't supposed to use them."

"Why did you touch it?"

"Because Mrs. Jackson was having trouble with it. She got up and walked away, so I went over to look at it. It had a bunch of names on it but they weren't lined up right. I thought I could fix it and hit a couple of keys just as Mr. Bloom walked in."

Mac figured he was on a roll, so he sidestepped a parental lecture regarding school property and instead asked casually, "Then what happened?"

"Mr. Bloom got mad and said I probably broke it. Then Mrs. Jackson came back in and said it was all fixed, and wasn't that a surprise. It wasn't to me," Davy muttered. "I knew it was okay."

Kat giggled and ruffled his hair. "Is Mr. Bloom the principal and Mrs. Jackson the secretary?"

Davy nodded. "Yeah."

"How did you know you could fix it?" she asked, keeping her tone carefully casual.

Davy shook his head, puzzled. "I don't know. I watched her a couple of times when I was in the office. It just seemed to make sense."

"Sometimes things work like that," Kat said easily.

Mac looked over at his son. "To answer your question, I won't get mad. And if it breaks, we'll just get it fixed. I know you well enough to realize you'd never deliberately damage that or anything else."

Davy smiled and leaned back in the seat, craning his neck to look out the window. The rest of the way into town, he kicked his heels against the seat and whistled softly to himself.

Kat wished she were as relaxed.

She might as well wish for the moon, or an entire colony of scentless skunks, she thought glumly. Although Mac still held her hand captive on his thigh, she knew if she tugged he would release her. When he had stated the terms of their agreement with such clarity—his assistance was the carrot offered and seduction was the goal—Mac hadn't needed to state the obvious. While he might employ sneaky tactics and charm the socks off her, he would never use force. And on some basic, instinctive level, she had known that and trusted him.

She still did.

Kat tentatively wiggled her fingers and he turned her hand, linking his fingers through hers. No, she thought again as he looked down at her with gleaming eyes, he wouldn't use force. He wouldn't have to. The man had an entire arsenal of pure attraction at his disposal.

Gazing at their hands, resting palm-to-palm on his thigh, she recalled his surprise when she had accepted his challenge so quickly. She had told him why, but he hadn't believed her. He'd learn soon enough, she thought complacently. Arsenal or no arsenal, the arrangement wasn't a one-way street.

He had been blunt when telling her what he wanted. But she found what he didn't want even more revealing. Mac didn't want a wife. Yet, from what she had observed in these few days, he seemed to find domestic life vastly satisfying. Sitting by a blazing fire at night, reading or playing a game with Davy, he had been the picture of a loving father. Only the searing glances he'd occasionally sent in her direction had reminded her that there was an element missing in the equation.

That night in the barn, when Mac had asked her if she was a gambler, she had told him truthfully that she preferred having the odds in her favor. But every now and then she went out on a limb, and that was precisely where she was now. She would be willing to wager an entire year's salary that Mac really did want a wife. That he'd like nothing more than to be a fully domesticated Wyoming rancher.

But he had been badly burned once and he was determined not to go near the flame again. She could understand his reaction. He was a man who took his responsibilities seriously, and his self-imposed prime duty seemed to be protecting everyone in his domain. If any of them met with misfortune or death, he was responsible. He had failed to do his duty.

What an incredible burden to carry, she thought, leaning back and closing her eyes. No wonder he wasn't willing to risk bringing another wife to the ranch. Especially one who was born in the city. He didn't want any more grief in his life and she couldn't blame him.

But she doubted if he would be satisfied living on the fringes much longer. Mac was a man with roots. According to Claude, the Ryders had been ranchers on the same land for over a hundred years. They had bred horses and cattle, married for love, had children and expected the next generation to do the same.

No, Mac wouldn't remain single forever, but she wouldn't be around to see his inevitable tumble into wedded bliss. Once she corralled enough skunks, she would be back in her lab attending to business, while her mother plotted with other desperate mamas of eligible bachelors.

In the meantime...

Kat grinned and leaned companionably against Mac. In the meantime, he would do his damnedest to seduce her, and she would undoubtedly be tempted. After all, what was not to like about Mackenzie Ryder? He was intelligent, had a good sense of humor, a killer smile and a body toughened by hard physical labor. A nifty combination if there ever was one.

Mac released her hand to drape his arm around her shoulders and tug her closer to the heat of his body. "You're awfully quiet all of a sudden. Everything okay?"

"Just fine. I'm thinking of ways to spend your money once we hit town," she lied, taking a quick upward peek to see if he believed her. Apparently he did.

"I'll drop you and Davy at the computer place, then pick up the supplies for the big skunk expedition. I'll meet you back there when I'm done."

"Sounds good. Give me enough time to spend a lot of money."

"You'll have to hustle because I won't be long. You know," he said softly, "as crazy as this skunk idea is, I'm looking forward to it."

Kat rolled her eyes. Of course he was. He was working under a major handicap at the ranch, what with Claude and Davy operating as built-in chaperons. Once out in the wilderness, she had no doubt that he would do exactly as he promised—help her with the skunks and do his darnedest to seduce her.

She was looking forward to the trip, too. For vastly different reasons, however. It had been far too long since she had participated in any fieldwork and now that she had someone to stand between her and the local wildlife, it could be a fascinating experience.

In more ways than one, she thought, gazing through the windshield. Over the last several years, she had been too preoccupied with her work to get involved with many men. Limited time meant limited experience. Most of her dates had been with men from work and had turned into marathon ecology discussions. Not exactly tabloid material, she thought wryly.

Mac was a whole different breed. Intensely male, shatteringly direct. She had never, ever dealt with a man like him. Kat blinked, thinking about the days—and nights— they would be spending together.

Then she thought about her ace in the hole, the second part. She had been honest with him—up to a point. She had told him that she wasn't a passionate woman. She had simply neglected to mention that three years earlier, after an awkward situation with a man she'd been dating, she had vowed never to sleep with a man that she didn't love.

Five

"**H**ave you ever used a dart gun before?"

Kat shook her head. "Nope. Never." Her gaze drifted away from Mac and she surveyed the neat campsite with satisfaction. Mac definitely had a talent for making order out of chaos, she decided. It was a trait she appreciated because it was exactly the way she ran her lab in Denver.

Only a couple of hours ago, after they had unloaded an alarming array of stuff from the shell of Mac's pickup, the place had looked like a war zone. Now a green tent housed a large inflated air mattress and sleeping bags along with clothes and other assorted necessities. Peeking inside, she had regarded the single mattress with raised brows, then shrugged. It looked comfortable and they did have separate bags. Any other consideration could be dealt with later.

A stove and insulated chest, scuffed and well used, lifted her spirits. If she had been alone, her provisions would have consisted of trail mix, dried fruit, cold cereal and powdered milk. But if the box of supplies still in the truck was any indication, Mac was not a man who believed in depriving himself where food was concerned. She had definitely lucked out on this venture, Kat reflected, surveying the loot with pleasure.

They were a three-hour drive from the ranch, at the high end of a long grassy valley, fifty feet or so from the edge of the forest. Tall pines stood like sentries, their huge branches casting dark shadows on the ground beneath them.

So far the outdoor life wasn't all that bad, she decided. The weather had done a complete turnaround, bringing sunshine and warm air currents that melted the snow and provided perfect temperatures for shorts and sleeveless shirts. Closing her eyes, Kat delicately sniffed the fragrant air. It was an intriguing mixture of pines and moist soil, wildflowers and heat.

She cocked her head, listening. Accustomed as she was to the demanding clamor of the city, it seemed shockingly silent at first. Then she heard the drone of a bee, a breeze murmuring through the trees and a pinecone blundering through branches to fall on the dry needles below. The cry of a hawk shrilled overhead, and water splashed sweetly in a nearby stream.

"Kat?"

She opened her eyes and saw Mac leaning against the back fender of his truck, holding the dart gun. He waggled it, bringing her back to the present with a jolt.

"Did I hear you right? Are you telling me you've never used this thing?"

Kat nodded. "Yep. But John said it was a snap," she assured him blithely.

He sighed and pushed away from the truck. Stopping in front of her, he gazed at her with an expression she was beginning to recognize. It fell somewhere between disbelief and resignation. "John happens to know what he's doing when he's out tracking down animals. You don't. That's why I'm here, remember? Have you ever shot *any* kind of a gun?'' he asked softly.

Kat grinned. She couldn't help it. She was also getting familiar with that soft voice. Usually the softer and slower he talked, the more trouble she was in. Unless he was yelling at her. That was trouble, too, but she had yet to figure out which was worse.

Mac's problem was that he took things too seriously, she decided. If he wasn't warning her about falling in a sealed well that she couldn't have pried open with TNT, he was fretting about her clothes and the possibility of frostbite. In town the other day, he had ushered her into the store and supervised every item she had bought—which had amused the salesclerk to no end. Some of the things she selected he tossed aside, discounting them as frivolous. Others he took from racks, thrust them into her arms and told her to take them—such as the ugly, round-toed boots with laces. Style and color hadn't been considerations. His entire focus had been on warmth and durability. She was now prepared for anything—with the possible exception of famine and a horde of locust.

And now the gun. She was surprised that he hadn't mentioned it before, when he'd grilled her about everything else and confirmed his original opinion that she was hopelessly inept when it came to camping. She had a strong hunch that she was about to receive a lecture on firearms.

''Guns don't rate very high with me,'' she conceded. ''I'm not exactly a fan of the NRA. I've never handled one—not even a squirt gun.'' She brightened. ''But there's nothing to worry about. There must be a zillion of those cartridge things for the dart gun, so if I miss once or twice it's no big deal.''

''Once or twice?''

''Whatever.''

Mac's voice grew even softer. "Odd as it may seem, some people actually practice on a stationary target before they try something that's moving."

"For heaven's sake, Mac, it's not as if I had months to prepare for this," she reminded him. "I only heard about John's mumps the day I was leaving." She gave him her best shot at an innocent smile. "Since my experience is so limited, it's a good thing that skunks don't move very fast, isn't it?"

He narrowed his eyes and put one hand on her shoulder. "Look, Annie Oakley, as long as I'm anywhere in the neighborhood, you're not waving a gun around that's loaded with a tranquilizer."

"It's safer than bullets."

"Just barely," he said dryly. "Especially in your hands. Have you given any thought to what could happen if you got me with one of those things and you ended up on your own?"

Kat eyed him assessingly, ignoring the last part of his statement. "I think the dosage is geared for a lot less body weight than yours. I doubt if you'd even get drowsy." She gave him another sunny smile. "So there's really no problem."

"You're damned right there isn't. Because you're not going to touch the thing. I'll do the shooting around here."

"My hero." She folded her hands over her heart and batted her lashes.

"Don't push it, lady. You look hard enough for trouble and you're liable to find it." He gave her a challenging grin and moved closer. His hands settled on her shoulders and he waited just long enough for her to protest. When she only widened her eyes in surprise, he lowered his head to brush his lips over hers.

Kat held her breath, tasting coffee and desire on his lips. One large hand slid down her back and tightened, drawing her hips against his. She leaned into him, letting him take her weight, her fingers twisting in his hair. He felt so good. Hard and solid and strong. So good.

"You feel so damn good," he muttered, his words echoing her thoughts.

Kat leaned back and took a shaky breath, giving him a stunned look. It wasn't the fact that he had kissed her, she thought, dazed. Once they left the ranch and the security of Claude and Davy's presence, she had more or less expected him to. Had been looking forward to it in a way, wondering if it would live up to the kiss they had shared in the hall that first night. No, the kiss wasn't the problem. It was the heat flooding her veins that shocked her, as well as the flutter of anticipation.

This wasn't supposed to happen, she told herself, turning her head to the side, away from his sharp gaze. She wasn't supposed to want Mac. This was all a game. A challenge.

And when it was over, the idea was to walk away intact, untouched. To go back to Denver, to the lab that had been equipped just for her, to the condo that, after a year, still wasn't completely furnished, and to her family. To go back where she wrapped the long hours of work around her like a cloak and convinced herself that her life was rich and complete.

Looking back at Mac, she blinked up at him uncertainly and wondered what they had been talking about before the ground had dropped out from under her feet. Whatever it was, it wasn't nearly as important as putting some space between them to break the sizzling connection.

She cautiously backed away, her gaze settling gratefully on the cases of syringes and vials for blood. "I thought we came here to find skunks," she said breathlessly. "Let's get the stuff and head for the trees."

"Wait a minute." He didn't try to tug her back. Instead,

he held up a hand, stopping her. "Not so fast. There are a few things I want to cover before we do that."

"Mac, we're wasting precious time." She glanced up at the sun. "It's already late afternoon. We have no idea how long the weather will stay this mild, and you know that once winter sets in for good, a skunk won't poke his nose out of the snow. If that happens, my work will be set back four or five months."

"You'll be worse off than that if you have an accident because we didn't talk about a few basic safety rules."

Kat groaned and looked heavenward. "Please," she said piously, "tell me he's kidding. Send down a lightning bolt, anything." She waited impatiently, and in vain. She reluctantly turned to Mac. "Tell me you didn't mean it. You're not talking about a crash course in wilderness training right now, are you?"

He was. She could tell it by the implacable look in his dark eyes. He simply stood there, smiling that killer smile, and she knew she didn't have a hope of changing his mind. "All right," she said, sighing, "we'll do it your way. Just remember, I'm a quick study. You can skip a lot of the preliminaries."

"Yeah, I have it on good authority that you're bright. We'll see just how sharp you are. But before we leave, you'd better change into something warmer. As soon as you step out of the sun, you'll get cool."

It was dinnertime before they returned. He led the way back to the truck and laid wood for a small fire while Kat pulled on a jacket. Within minutes the fire was blazing, and he set up a grill over the flames, whistling softly as he worked.

"Are you hungry?"

"Yes." It was the truth. She *was* hungry—as well as tired and annoyed. Dammit, she was here to work. He had

acted like a park ranger all afternoon, pointing out trees
and shrubs and telling her more than she'd ever wanted to
know about nature in general. Actually, she admitted, it had
been fairly interesting. It would have been downright fascinating if she hadn't been so anxious about the passing
hours. Fortunately they hadn't spotted a single skunk on
the prowl, so the issue hadn't become more charged than
it already was.

"I'm starved," she confessed.

"Good. There are a couple of steaks in the cooler. Will
you get them for me?"

She handed him the steaks and moved out of his way.
Mac cooked over a campfire as easily as he did everything
else, she noted absently, wondering if he was going to insist
she learn how to do that, as well, before they got down to
business with the skunks. If he valued his skin, he wouldn't
try.

She had followed him for miles today, absorbing the information he passed on. Giving him another disgruntled
glance, she reluctantly admitted that he was a good teacher.
She had learned to note landmarks, how to mark a trail,
how to look for water and find the way out of the forest.
He had even covered the delicate issue of answering nature's call without getting eaten alive by chiggers. She had
no intention of getting into a situation that called for any
of the lessons—except the last one—as long as she was
with him.

Walking over to the back of the truck, she leaned in and
poked around. Looking up with a pleased smile, she said,
"Hey, we've got all the comforts of home here." She
pulled out a collapsed card table and two folding chairs and
set them up.

Mac slanted a teasing glance at her. "Yeah, city slickers
need a certain amount of spoiling."

"Good. Let's hear it for coddling the greenhorns. Did

you stash a shower and hot water in here?'' She took another peek inside.

"No, but in that small box you'll find some plastic plates and silverware.''

She set the table, then straddled a chair near the fire and watched him. "Ah, this is the life," she sighed, folding her hands on the chair back and propping her chin on them. "By the way, if I didn't mention it, I like my steak well done.''

Mac shook his head. "Don't you people in the city know how to eat good meat?''

"People in the city have heard about things like salmonella and E. coli,'' she retorted. "Well-done, please.''

"Whatever you say, Ms. Genius.''

"That's Doctor Genius, if you don't mind.''

He took his gaze off the steaks long enough to glance at her in surprise. "I'm impressed. When did that happen?''

"When I was twenty-three.'' She shrugged. "I moved through my classes pretty fast.''

"Did you ever have any trouble handling it?''

"Being smart, you mean?''

He nodded, stooping to turn the potatoes on the grill.

"You're anxious about Davy, aren't you?'' Kat saw the concern in his dark eyes and knew the question was ridiculous. Of course he was worried. "My parents made sure I understood that I had been given a gift, much like someone with perfect pitch or artistic talent. I couldn't get a big head over something like that, could I?''

"What about other problems?''

She gazed out across the valley, remembering. "They were primarily social,'' she said finally. "I wasn't a normal teenager, if there is such a thing. My mind was reaching out in too many directions for me to be interested in dating.''

She gave him an amused look. "I was probably a nerd.

But if I was, I never realized it. I had friends, we kept ourselves entertained, and I was happy. Davy will be fine,'' she assured him, passing him the plates. ''There are plenty of things to do on a ranch that will bring him back to earth when he gets lost in his head.''

Mac flipped the steaks onto the plates, added the potatoes and some green beans and moved to the table. Kat cut a bite-sized piece of the meat and popped it into her mouth.

''Oh, God,'' she said reverently a moment later. ''Even if you couldn't shoot a gun, you'd be worth a fortune as a cook. Remind me to give you a raise.''

''You're not paying me anything,'' he reminded her. ''At least, not in cash.''

''Not in anything else, either.''

''Yet.'' He grinned at her look of exasperation. ''Today's just the first day.''

Kat tried quelling him with a frown, then realized what she already knew on some broader instinctive level—Mackenzie Ryder was not a man easily quelled.

She leaned back and forked up another piece of steak. Chewing was simply an action to mask her jangling nerves, a delaying device. She hadn't been kidding when she told him about her awkward social life, but she had rather glossed over the worst parts. On that particular plane, she had definitely lagged behind her peers. Each time she emerged from the academic heights she had found so stimulating, she had felt more inept and out of place.

On a social level, the university had been just as disastrous. In every other way it had been sheer heaven. To participate in projects with some of the finest minds in the ecology field had been an unparalleled joy. It had given her a sense of self-worth that not even a series of dead-end dates and a couple of sputtering affairs could destroy.

When she had been courted by and eventually hired by Dan Matlock's privately funded environmental firm, she learned that a fast line of patter could cover up most awkward situations. And, she reflected with devastating honesty, it wasn't necessary to do that too often. Most of the men in her life were the ones she worked with, and they were usually too intimidated by her IQ and her position in the company to be much of a problem. Most of them, in fact, were as dedicated as she was, too preoccupied with their work to see her as more than another person in the brain pool.

So the months had stretched into years. Most of the men she encountered either became friends or passed out of her life. The few times she had ventured into more intimate relationships had not been raging successes.

But never had she encountered a man like Mac Ryder. Tall, massive as the mountains surrounding his ranch, eyes gleaming with the heat of a banked fire, he was a living, breathing prototype of masculine sensuality. And he wanted her.

The idea was mind-boggling.

If she were only a living, breathing prototype of feminine sensuality, she would feel better about the whole thing. But she wasn't, and she never would be, so she'd better do some fast thinking. That was the one thing she was really good at, she reminded herself. Thinking.

There was just one major problem. Her mind seemed stuck on the fact that she was reacting to him in a manner that was completely foreign to her. He excited her. When she thought about the desire gleaming in the depths of his eyes, she got a major case of butterflies. He made her feel as nervous as a young girl going on her first big date.

Kat blinked thoughtfully. That was a problem. She did a lot of things very well, but dating wasn't one of them. Even when it was called by another name—affair, relationship, whatever—it all boiled down to the same thing. It was a bonding, an ever-deepening connection that had one ultimate goal. And intimacy was another thing she didn't do very well. Brian had been her last attempt, and after a couple of weeks they had parted with no regrets on either side.

However... Kat brightened. One thing she was a whiz at was friendship. If she could just redirect his focus a bit...

Kat cleared her throat. "Speaking of Davy," she began casually.

"Were we?" Mac murmured. "Funny, I thought we were—"

"Probably one of the reasons he's up all hours of the night is because he hasn't been challenged mentally during the day," she said hastily. "I used to drive my parents crazy doing the same thing. I think you'll see a big difference once he gets involved with some of the software you paid for."

"Kat—"

"He needs to be challenged," she said, plowing on determinedly. "And that's exactly what all those programs were designed to do."

"Ah."

"They weren't making them when I was his age, so my parents had to hustle to find things for me. Kids these days are lucky."

"Yeah." Mac cut off a piece of bleeding meat and chewed it, gazing at her blandly.

"And then, of course, there's the testing. Once the school in Denver calls and you get it done, you'll feel better."

"I will?"

"Sure. You'll know exactly where Davy places and what you can do for him. The hard part is when you don't know what the status is."

"Right."

"And I'll help any way I can. My nephew, Cody, is just

three years older than Davy, so I became familiar with a lot of the new programs available.''

''That's handy.''

''Will you *stop* it?'' Kat dropped her fork on her plate and glared at him. ''I'm just trying to help.''

Mac tilted his head and studied her flustered expression. ''Is that what you call it? Sounded to me like you were trying to change the subject.''

''I was not!''

''Could have fooled me,'' he said with a shrug. ''Look, Kat, I don't know what you're so antsy about all of a sudden, but why don't we just try a little honesty here?''

''Honesty?'' She repeated the word cautiously, as if she were hearing it for the first time. ''Okay, you first.''

''All right. I want you so much I ache, and I'm pretty damn sure you want me.'' He picked up her hand and smoothed his thumb over her fingers, ignoring her restless movement. ''But something's going on here, and I'm no good at reading between the lines. Whatever it is, you don't have to use Davy as a shield. If the thought of sleeping with me turns you off, just say so.''

''Good grief,'' Kat muttered. She tugged at her hand, but his tightened fractionally and held it. He wasn't hurting her so she gave up the uneven struggle. ''Are you always this blunt with...''

''My bed partners?'' Mac thumbed back the brim of his hat a notch. ''Yeah, I am. First of all, things are pretty straightforward on a ranch. You learn early on to call a spade a spade. On top of that, I'm not a romantic. I never learned how to pretty things up. And finally, in this day and age, it's too dangerous not to be honest. I haven't been with a woman in months, and I had a physical a few weeks ago. I'm healthy and safe.'' He waited, eyeing her expectantly.

"So am I," she mumbled, avoiding his gaze. "Healthy, I mean. And safe."

Mac looked puzzled at her grudging reply. "You're embarrassed," he said finally, giving her a half grin.

Kat rolled her eyes. "Let me tell you something, Mackenzie Ryder. When it comes to dealing with women, you have all the sensitivity of that hunk of rock over there." She waved at a distant mountain.

"If you're not comfortable having a conversation like this with the men in your life, then you'd better dump them or head for a convent," he said bluntly, frowning at her.

"There haven't been that many. Lately," she added hastily. "I've more or less lost touch with proper protocol."

"Why?" He seemed genuinely curious.

Kat frowned. "Why, what?"

"Why haven't there been? Many men. Lately. You're beautiful, sexy as hell. What's the matter with them?"

Kat was not about to discuss her inadequacies—especially with a man who had just called her beautiful and sexy. Lifting her shoulders in a slight shrug, she gave him an answer that was at least partially true. "I don't have a nine-to-five job. Men in other fields won't put up with my long hours."

"What about the men you work with?"

She shook her head. "Maybe we see too much of each other at work. Maybe we're too much alike. I don't know."

"Just for the record, we don't have any of those problems," Mac informed her, releasing her hand. "Come on, let's get the dishes done. From now on, I'll do the cooking if you'll do the cleanup."

"It's a deal."

They collected the dishes, and she followed him to the stream. Mac demonstrated how to scour them with the sand at the edge of the water while she watched.

"Now that's a handy trick." Kat took a plate from him and dried it. "And there's no soap to ruin the water."

"Country people have been taking care of their land for several hundred years." Mac handed her the knives and forks. "Outsiders are the problem. Like tourists who leave their trash, and trucks looking for a nice quiet place to dump toxic waste."

Kat looked up with a frown. "Do you have much of that?"

"Not now. Had a bad incident a couple of years ago."

"What happened?"

Mac gave her a grim smile. "We formed a posse, complete with helicopters and radios. When we caught them, the state cracked down on the companies involved and put them out of business. Now we keep an eye on things."

"Good." Kat patted him on the arm. "It's nice to know that while I'm trying to save the world, people are keeping the bad guys in line."

"Yeah, we do our best."

Kat replaced the dishes in the box, sliding it into the back of the truck. "And speaking of my work, when do we get started? The clock is ticking, remember?"

Mac nodded. "I know. We'll turn in early, sleep until three or four and go looking for your friends. It'll be chilly, but we'll have a better chance of finding them then than we would during the day."

"Good. I'll give the equipment one last check. Oh—" She turned and gave him a teasing glance. "Are you sure there aren't any dire warnings you forgot this afternoon? If there are, now's the time to mention them."

"Yeah." He ambled closer. "There is one thing. If you run into a grizzly when I'm not around, don't try to run. They can move a hell of a lot faster than you can."

"Thanks," she said faintly. "And what if one comes by tonight?"

"If you're smart, you'll be worrying about something else."

"What?"

Mac grinned. "Me."

Six

"Good grief, that cough is terrible," Kat muttered sleepily. She removed her hand from the downy warmth that cocooned her and nudged the cold, smooth surface of the sleeping bag next to hers. "Don't you have anything you can take?"

Mac turned toward her. "Quiet," he breathed.

"Me?" Her eyes snapped open. "I'm not the one making all the racket." She flounced onto her back, grumbling. "All I said was—" A hand, hard and warm, clamped over her mouth, cutting off any further comments. The hand was followed by a dark shape leaning over her, a denser mass of black in the already inky tent.

"It's not me making the noise." Mac's whisper was barely audible. "We've got company."

"Hmm?" she hummed against his hand.

"A bear."

"*Mmfph.*" Kat stiffened and locked her hand around his

wrist, trying to push it away. Her struggle was not only useless, it seemed to provoke him. Mac rolled over on her, holding her still with the weight of his body.

"Not a word." His warning contained only a thread of sound. "I mean it. Will you be quiet if I move my hand?"

Kat nodded, sighing when he slid his palm over to cup her cheek. She tugged his head down close to hers and whispered shakily into his ear. "What's it doing out there?"

Mac turned her face away and grazed her earlobe with his teeth, grinning when she gasped. "Looking for food, I imagine."

"Stop that," she hissed, pushing on his shoulder. He didn't so much as twitch, she noted with annoyance. That is, until he let his weight rest more fully on her, pushing her deeper into the air mattress. "This is serious," she hissed. "*Do* something! Do you have a gun with you?"

It was too dark to see a thing, but she felt the patient look he turned on her. Of course he had a gun. This was the man who was prepared for all eventualities. She had no doubt that it was right beside him, loaded and ready to use. Still...

"You *do* have it in here, don't you?" she whispered. When he didn't respond quickly enough, she added, "Tell me it's not—"

"Will...you...for...God's...sake...be...quiet?" he said through clenched teeth. "Yes, the damn rifle is right next to me, but I don't want to use it unless I have to. If you'll just be still, he'll get bored and go away."

Kat relaxed, then stiffened when a new worry hit her. "We didn't leave any food out, did we? I can't remember if I put everything away? What if I—" Mac's hand clamped over her mouth again, muffling the words against his palm.

"Everything's put away," he muttered. "Now, for God's

sake, be still.'' He swore and jerked his hand away when Kat opened her mouth and nipped the fleshy part of his finger. ''Dammit, woman, you bite me again, and we're going to do some serious talking. Come here.''

With a swiftness that took Kat by surprise, he rolled to his side, eased back the top of his sleeping bag and reached for her. Wrapping his arm around her waist, he tugged her against him.

One large hand shaped her head, pressing her face against his bare chest. When her lips parted, his grip tightened around her waist. ''Don't even think about it,'' he warned softly, thinking of the nip she'd given his finger.

''What are you doing?'' She kept her frantic question low this time, remembering their prowling visitor. ''I can't breathe!''

''You're still talking,'' he muttered in exasperated amusement, ''so I don't think it's a big problem.''

Kat thumped him on his shoulder with a closed fist. ''This isn't funny. If you need that blasted gun, how can you get to it when we're all squashed in like this?''

''Relax.'' Mac's arms closed around her and he rolled to his back, groaning with pleasure when she sprawled across him. He soothed a hand down her elegant spine and cupped her lush bottom, flexing his fingers.

He had given her a few minutes alone in the tent before he'd joined her, and she had donned an outsize T-shirt before she'd crawled into bed. The hem was now tangled around her waist. Below it was the skimpiest piece of silk he'd ever had the good fortune to feel.

Her skin felt like satin against him. Resilient. Tempting. Inviting. Soft. Yeah, it figured. She was soft as silk, and he was hard as a rock.

''*Relax?*'' Kat repeated in a strangled voice, trying to find a safe place to put her hands.

''Shh.'' Mac's other hand framed her head, drawing it

down to rest on his chest. "Just be still and listen to our friend out there."

Kat listened. The bear circled the tent several times, its grunts sounding eerily like a human's cough. Kat stiffened, digging her fingers into Mac's shoulders when it brushed by them, its coat rasping against the coarse cloth of the tent wall.

A good imagination wasn't always a blessing, she reflected nervously, picturing the huge animal rearing on its hind legs, slashing its claws through the fragile fabric barrier.

A good memory fell in the same dismal category. She remembered quite clearly how Mac had described a grizzly. One could weigh over a thousand pounds and stand as tall as nine or ten feet. Not a pleasant thought, especially when she was locked, half naked and more vulnerable than she had ever imagined being, in a sleeping bag with a man who claimed he had a gun. Somewhere.

"Damn."

The soft whisper jolted her. She raised her head and looked around frantically. "What?"

"Listen to him. He's scratching the hell out of my truck."

She tensed, trying to hear, and realized with a jolt of relief that Mac was right. The bear had moved away from the tent. She thought it a small enough sacrifice—a few scratches on a truck compared to a gaping hole in the tent—but refrained from saying so. Men had a tendency to be unreasonable when it came to their trucks, especially when the vehicle was as new as Mac's.

Sighing, Kat relaxed against Mac, letting him take her weight. Slowly awareness of something other than the terrifying animal prowling around their campsite seeped into her consciousness. For the first time she realized that Mac was wearing nothing but knit briefs. His powerfully built body, overwhelmingly male, radiated enough heat to warm the entire tent.

And he was hard. All over.

"I think he's giving up," Mac said. "Sounds like he's going away."

Kat blew out a shaky breath of relief. "It's about time." It was also time for her to move, she decided. What with an enormous bear scaring her witless, she had had all she could cope with for one night. She definitely wasn't up to dealing with a near naked, sexy rancher.

She gave a tentative wiggle, trying to shift to Mac's side. He groaned and stopped her with his hands on her bottom, holding her in place.

"Mac?" She hesitated then went on. "I don't think this is a good idea."

"Relax, Doc." He ran a hand slowly down to her knee then back up again, sliding it to the inside of her thigh. "There's nothing to worry about."

"I'm not so sure about that." Her voice was shaky, and she tensed, concentrating on the path his trailing fingers were taking, waiting for them to glide to a halt at the most vulnerable part of her body. Instead, they reversed direction and drifted back toward her knee. Letting out her pent-up breath, Kat moved restlessly. "I think I'll just get back in my sleeping bag."

Mac's hands tightened on the back of her thighs. "Not yet, Doc. I just got an idea. Don't know why I didn't think of it before."

Kat braced herself at the sound of his teasing voice. It was a side of him she had seen only when he was with Davy. She hesitated, curiosity battling with caution. "All right," she finally said. "I'll bite. What?"

"Let's forget all about the bear and pretend we're in a parked car."

Kat blinked in the darkness, baffled. "Why on earth would we do that?"

Mac gave a wry groan. *Because I love to torture myself.* "You weren't kidding when you said you skipped a lot in your teens. Everybody knows what you do in a parked car." His hands slid up to the curve of her buttocks. "We can't have you going through life missing something like that."

"It's a little late to worry about it," she said dryly. "That was a long time ago."

"You're missing the point, Doc." There was a smile in his voice. "We pretend. I'm a sixteen-year-old kid out with a girl whose daddy is waiting at home with a loaded shotgun. I know the boundaries, and I know we're not going to cross them. But—"

"There's always a *but*," Kat commented, folding her arms on his chest and resting her chin in her hands. Trying to ignore the fact that he was all but naked beneath her, she waited to hear the rest of his preposterous idea. For a man who had said he was only interested in a hot, short-term affair with no strings attached, he was approaching the matter in a strangely roundabout way.

"But, there's a lot of leeway between the starting line and the finish," he added.

Kat's brows rose. "The finish being the boundary you don't cross because Daddy will shoot off your, ah, toes?"

"Right." He sounded pleased that she understood.

"And the girl? What does she know?"

"The same stuff. Daddy, the shotgun, the finish line."

Sighing, Kat wondered just where he was heading. She suspected that Mac didn't often drop into a good old boy routine, so it was undoubtedly for her benefit. And instinct told her that helping her forget about the bear wasn't the only reason for the elaborate scenario.

"So, keeping Daddy, his shotgun and all the rest in mind, what are we doing in a parked car?"

"Doc." He sighed mournfully and held her tighter. "You're not trying. Think. Use that famous brain for something beside plans to irritate some skunks."

"Okay, I've got it." She propped her elbows on his chest and looked down, even though she couldn't make out his features. "We pulled off the road, found a secluded spot and we're going to push the boundaries a bit. But not so much that Daddy brings out the gun," she finished.

"Bingo." He sounded pleased. "Doc, you have definite possibilities. Now here's the plan, but remember, you have to use your imagination just a bit," he warned. "This is our parked car, and you get to go back in time and make up for a few of the things you missed in your deprived youth."

Kat blinked. "And what do you do?

"I go along for the ride." Blatant satisfaction deepened his voice. "To take care of you, of course."

Kat took a shallow breath, her mind working at a furious pace. Mac was displaying a degree of sensitivity she had not expected in such a rugged mountain of a man.

In a few teasing words he had managed to both reassure her and make her pulse flutter with anticipation. He was seducing her and making no secret of the fact. He was also telling her she had nothing to fear, that she was safe with him—at least for tonight.

And knowingly or not, he had appealed to her lively sense of curiosity. She had been a young sixteen when she graduated from high school. Too young and far too innocent to socialize with her classmates when she moved up to the university. Too intimidated and too frightened.

She had bypassed the entire dating process, had never experienced the gradual emergence of her femininity, never witnessed the effect of its power on young men. In short, she had lost chunks of a normal life and had been expected to slide right into the adult singles scene. It hadn't worked very well.

Mac waited, hardly daring to breathe. He was terrified that one false move would remind her that she was sprawled all over him. He had never wanted a woman the way he wanted Kat, and he had just promised that he would not rush her. And he would honor that promise, even if it killed him.

And it just might, but he was willing to take the risk. He wanted Kat in his arms, tasting him, moving against him, holding him as if she would never let him go. And if he had to tease the elusive genius into doing it, as well as promise her safety, then that's what he would do.

His hands were at Kat's waist, holding her against him, but she was thinking so hard he doubted that she noticed. She would take the bait, he was sure of it. He had seen the sensual curiosity in her gorgeous blue eyes when she watched him. Had seen the feminine speculation. She wanted him, he thought with satisfaction. Wanted him badly, but was either too inexperienced, too inhibited—or both—to do anything about it. He knew it because with her expressive face and eyes she didn't have a hope in hell of concealing her feelings.

And there was another thing. The luscious, brainy doctor may have slept with men, but he was certain she hadn't received a lot of satisfaction doing it. He was also certain that she had no idea what had been lacking.

That was going to be his job, Mac promised himself. It would be his privilege to show Kat just what she had been missing. If he lived long enough.

Just as he began to wonder if he had miscalculated and rushed her, Kat relaxed against him and he had the feeling that the issue had been resolved. He held his breath until she nuzzled her cheek against his chest.

"I've always liked convertibles," she said softly.

Mac touched his fingers to her dark cloud of hair. "You're in luck. That's exactly what we have."

"Red?"

"Of course."

Waiting, Mac smiled, wondering what she'd come up with next. Suggesting this had been a stroke of brilliance, he decided complacently. Because, in spite of her interest in him, Kat would never have made the first move—and she would have been decidedly leery about any action on his part.

"Mac?"

"Yeah?" He waited, promising himself again that he wouldn't rush her.

"We're parked near a lake, okay? All by ourselves?"

He splayed his hand over the curve of her hip. "Sounds good to me."

"What do we do next?"

"I thought you'd never ask."

He rolled to his side, taking Kat with him. The key word here is *control,* he reminded himself as her hair slid in a silky cloud over his shoulder, tendrils clinging to his chest. Control, he thought vaguely as her head settled on his arm and he leaned over her. Nice and easy, no rush. He brushed his lips over hers. Figuring her sigh was as good an invitation as he was going to get, he covered her mouth with his again. She slid her arms around his neck with a soft little sound that drove him crazy.

Gentle as the kiss was, he knew it jolted Kat. He felt her response in the tremor that worked through her body. Since she was pressed against him all the way down to her toes, the shiver imprinted his whole body. It also played merry hell with his control.

He wanted Kat. He wanted the tenderness and passion that shimmered in her. He wanted her humor, her lively intelligence, her uncertainty, her determination. He wanted it all.

And right now he wanted her body against his, flesh to flesh, no barriers between them. He slid his hand beneath the cotton shirt, working it up. Bracing himself on his forearm, he gave a tug and pulled the shirt over her head.

"Mackenzie Ryder," Kat gasped, "were you doing that when you were sixteen?"

He folded her back in his arms and dropped a light kiss on her mouth. "Not a chance. But we're filling in your past, not mine—and I have a feeling that you were always in accelerated classes. Weren't you, Doc?"

"True," she said breathlessly. "I was a good student." Her voice broke when he slid his hand down her bare back. "But I never had a class like this." He stopped at her hip and his fingers traced the scrap of silk. "Mac." It was a startled warning.

He ignored it. With another quick lift and a tug, he got rid of that, too. "Now, I know you're a fast learner, Doc, but I think we'll take a few minutes here for a little review."

The kiss began gently enough, but her response made him forget he had been teasing in an effort to reassure her. When Kat wound her arms around his neck, he forgot everything except the feel of her breasts nudging his chest, her nipples poking against him like hard berries.

She moaned against his lips, managing to combine surprise and a sensual hunger in the soft sound. Mac wanted to hear it again. And again. And again. He slid a hand to her bottom and pulled her close, pressing her hips against him, against the knit cotton fabric he wore, the only thing standing between her soft curves and the heated length of his arousal. One barrier left, he thought, and if he was going to honor his word to Kat, it would have to stay right where it was.

Mac lifted his head and smiled at her mutter of complaint. "Hold on, Doc." His husky whisper was a caress, a promise of more to come.

Moving both hands to her waist, he shifted her higher, high enough so his lips could slide along the curve of her breasts and wrap around the tight berries that were driving him crazy.

"Mac!" Her gasp, was a breathy sound. Startled. Excited. He smiled against the silky curves and trailed his tongue over her nipple, tightening his hold on her waist when her response was a quick shiver.

"How we doing, Doc?" he murmured against her skin. She didn't reply, at least not in words. But her body moved against his in a message as old as time. More, it said. More. Don't stop.

He didn't. He eased her to her back, supporting her head with his arm. Leaning over her, he shaped her breast with his hand. She was doing fine, one part of his mind noted absently. The night had turned cold, but the blood roaring through her veins was keeping her warm. He bent his head to kiss the pebbled bead cresting her breast. Yeah, she was just fine.

But he was in big trouble. He had been aroused before he'd pulled her into his arms—just the thought of her being next to him had done the trick. Holding her in his arms hadn't eased the situation any. Well, he knew his age hadn't done a damn thing for his control, he reflected with disgust. He was just as hot as a frustrated sixteen-year-old in a parked car.

Well, that was tough. Tonight had nothing to do with him, he reminded himself. It was for Kat. Nothing was as important as letting her discover her own feminine power, as bringing her the kind of satisfaction she should have been having for years.

Kat stirred, stretching languorously as his tongue stroked

first one nipple then the other. As his big hand dipped down
the hollow of her waist and settled on the mound near the
apex of her thighs, she stilled. Tension gripped her when
his thumb brushed through the silky dark hair.

"Mac?"

"Hush, Doc. You're doing just fine."

"I think—"

He cut her off at the beginning of her breathless protest.
"Don't think," he murmured. "Just feel."

"But—"

"There's nothing to worry about. I'm taking care of
you."

Mac lowered his hand and cut off whatever she was
about to say. When he touched her, her body arched, grew
taut. The soft sounds she made as he gently stroked were
electrifying. The helpless catch of her breath when he found
the tightly drawn feminine bud of sensation made him
harder than ever.

"Mac!" Her whisper shimmered with excitement and a
tinge of anxiety.

"Easy," he soothed. "I've got you. You're okay."

"No." When she shook her head, her hair tumbled over
his arm. "You don't...understand."

Mac dropped a kiss on one erect nipple while he traced
a light design on the vulnerable flesh now slick with her
own moisture.

"Understand what, Doc?"

"It's never been like... *Oh.* Stop. I can't..."

"Yes, you can," he whispered. "And you will."

But she wasn't trying to pull away, Mac realized as he
drew her nipple deeper into his mouth. She was lifting her
hips, pressing against his hand, wanting more. She wasn't
thinking now, she was simply responding as a woman on
the brink of something cataclysmic. Her body drew taut
again and she stilled, as if listening to something deep

within. A tremor shook Kat, then another one, and another, a series of sensual ripples taking her by storm.

"Mac." Brokenly, she cried his name as she turned into his arms, her body trembling against his.

Mac held her, waiting for the tremors to abate, wishing he could have seen her face. Then he recalled the soft sounds she had made in the darkness as she turned and twisted in his arms and knew that nothing could have been more thrilling.

Several minutes later Kat took a long, shaky breath and slumped against him, allowing her slim hand to drift over his chest and shoulder. "Mac?"

"Hmm?" He settled one hand on her hip to keep her from moving as he eased back a couple of inches. Control was once again a rising problem, he reflected grimly, and he didn't know how much more he could take of her soft body pressing against him.

"I'm not a bit sorry I didn't do this when I was sixteen." Her breath puffed against his shoulder as she whispered.

Mac tensed. Her reaction has been unmistakable, but had he somehow failed? Had he frightened her? Had he misunderstood what she had said earlier? "Why?" The question had to be asked even if he didn't want to hear her reply.

She smiled against his arm. "I could never have appreciated it then."

Mac released his breath and tried to keep some space between them when Kat snuggled closer.

"Mac?"

"Yeah?"

Kat yawned. "Another reason I'm not sorry is because I probably would have messed up my life by becoming an unwed mother." Her sleepy words ended on another yawn.

Mac stiffened. "If you had been with me, you wouldn't have ended up unwed," he informed her grimly.

Kat chuckled and patted his shoulder. "Well, I wouldn't have been with you, because I've never been in Wyoming until now."

Directing a scowl at the tent ceiling, Mac told himself that she was half asleep and didn't know what she was saying. It didn't matter. He still didn't like the idea of her being with another man—at any age. He also reminded himself that a man who wanted no long-term relationship, no commitments, no marriage, had no right to feel that way.

That didn't seem to matter, either. He was in the middle of reminding himself exactly why he didn't want any commitments when Kat spoke again.

"Mac?"

"What?"

"I never knew..."

He stroked her shoulder, touched by the wonder in her voice. "Knew what?"

She yawned and moved her head to his shoulder. "That it could be like that. It was the first time I... Thank you."

Seven

"**A** first, huh?"

It was a couple of hours before dawn, and they were sitting next to each other on a fallen tree where they had been silently waiting for a skunk to appear.

Kat scowled at him. "Don't push it, Ryder."

"Who, me?" His innocent look would have done credit to an angel.

"I don't see anyone else around here."

"Yeah, I guess you got a point."

Kat scooted to her right, putting a couple more inches between them.

"You keep doing that and you're going to fall off the end," he said mildly, glancing at the growing space between his hips and hers.

"I'm fine." Right. *Shell-shocked* might be a better word.

"You always this testy in the morning?"

"Yes." Especially when she had made a fool of herself the night before.

"I don't think so. I think something's bothering you. Like maybe last night. Want to talk about it?"

Kat slanted a look at him, wondering if he had ever heard of the word tact. "No."

"Why not?"

"Because." Because she still couldn't believe she had joined him in his sleeping bag and let him take off her clothes. Because she was still shaky from the tumultuous emotions that had torn through her. Because, afterward, when she had lain limp and exhausted in his arms she had still wanted more.

And now he wanted to sit here and *talk* about it?

No way. She had tucked the experience away, somewhere deep within her, to savor, to think about, and she was damn sure not going to sit on a log, wearing ugly, brown, round-toed boots with laces and discuss it as calmly as she would the weather.

Mercifully Mac had been dressed and outside the tent when he had called to wake her. She hadn't the foggiest idea how he had levered himself out of the sleeping bag without disturbing her, but she would be forever grateful that they had avoided a face-to-face morning after. If her luck held, she would avoid any more embarrassing encounters for the remainder of the trip.

Mac changed the subject. "You warm enough?"

"I'm fine. You were right about the clothes," she said, determined to be fair. "They are warm." Ugly but warm. The boots were only the beginning. There were also flannel-lined jeans, an insulated top, wool shirt, fleece jacket, hat and gloves.

"Good." He gave her a sharp glance and seemed satisfied. "So tell me again, exactly why are we sitting out here waiting for skunks?"

"Aside from the fact that you're out here because you're betting I'll fall into your bed before I get all the samples I need? It'll never happen, cowboy, but I'm willing to take all the help I can get." Kat closed her eyes in disgust, not believing she had uttered the very words that could lead them back to the one subject she was trying to dodge.

"Yeah." His glance was a lot warmer this time. "Aside from that."

"Animal anomalies," she said briskly.

"I remember that part. Two-headed cows and albino horses, right?"

She nodded. "And possibly scentless skunks."

Mac shifted to a more comfortable position. "Why do we care? I've lived out here all my life, and I can't see that it makes any difference whether they smell or not."

"You've got a point," Kat admitted. "I can only tell you why *I* care. Why scientists care." She looked at him and got an encouraging nod.

"I don't know exactly where to start with this," she began, leaning against a thick branch. "Maybe with our lab. We have sort of an ecological think tank, and we cover a number of related areas. For instance, some of us are studying disasters such as oil spills, some are working with groups cleaning lakes and streams. The list is almost endless."

"And what are you working on?"

"Right now, adaptability. See, the ideal situation would be to clear the air and water, enrich the soil and have a perfectly balanced world. But what if that can't be done? What if we ultimately have to live with a certain amount of pollution? How do we do it?"

"I'll bite. How?"

"By learning about the things that exist right now—like which trees can survive in a smog belt, which ones are dying and what makes the difference."

Mac folded his arms across his chest, concealing a sigh. He had guessed right. Doctor Kathryn Wainwright was an idealist, a bone-deep do-gooder. It was all right there, the dedication and excitement gleaming in her light blue eyes.

The world needed such people, there was no doubt about it, but he had mixed feelings about the subject. Hell, he had mixed feelings about *her*. His gaze rested on her lips and he forgot about her brainpower, forgot that she was the one qualified person he knew who could help Davy. Instead, he remembered the touch of her lips, soft and moist, on his. He remembered the muffled urgency of her cries as she climbed all over him.

Jerking himself back to the problem at hand, he thought about her job, the situation that had brought her here. He was like everyone else, he reflected. He wanted his part of the country to stay just the way it was, with clean air and tall healthy trees, workable land to be passed on to his children and their children. What he didn't want was a zealot discovering something that would result in thousands of acres being set aside as a preserve. It was the age-old argument between people who worked the land and those who wanted to save it.

"So where do the skunks come in?" he persisted.

"Well, it's all speculative right now, you understand. Maybe nothing will come of it." Her shrug was offhanded, but the gleam in her narrowed eyes said she wouldn't easily dismiss the possibility.

"The idea behind it goes something like this," she continued. "*If* there is a colony of scentless skunks, and if their scent glands are the same as the regular skunks, then the difference is more than likely genetic. The blood samples and DNA typing will show if there is actually a genetic difference." She paused, watching him expectantly.

Mac waited. When she didn't continue, he shook his head. "I'm right back to my original question. Who cares?

What's so important about finding whether there's a difference?''

"Oh." Kat blinked. "I guess I skipped over that part. The theory gets pretty iffy, but a change in an animal could indicate the possibility of a change in humans somewhere down the road. It's a feasibility that we have to investigate."

Her eyes were bright with the fervent zeal of a true crusader. "We study animals because of their short life spans and their breeding capabilities. They show changes much more quickly than humans, you know. So what it boils down to is if animals are changing genetically, it may be happening so they can better adapt to something in the area."

Mac nodded thoughtfully. "Which could mean that people might change genetically in generations to come, and that drops the whole ball of wax in your domain."

"Bingo." She grinned. "Adaptability."

"What if it doesn't pan out?"

Kat tilted her head, studying him. "You mean, if we find nothing at all?"

"Yeah."

"Well, it won't be a terrible setback or major financial loss," she said pragmatically. "I'll lose some vacation time and the lab will be out money for the testing."

Mac reached out with unexpected swiftness and wrapped his arm around her waist. Scooping her up and settling her next to him, he said, "Come on, Doc, this is me you're talking to, not a reporter or someone financing the thing. I know better than that. You want this to work out so bad you can taste it."

She grabbed his hand to steady herself and looked up, eyes blazing with excitement. "It all goes back to what I said before—adaptability. A skunk's scent is its major defense mechanism. If there are skunks out here surviving without it, it could mean that they've developed another form of defense. And that could mean...all sorts of exciting things!"

He had been right, Mac thought with resignation. She was out to save the world. And nothing would stop her. Not time, not money, not her own stamina. Nothing.

"Well, in that case," he said with a sigh, "I guess we'd better find some skunks for you, Doc. Did you get any useful information from John? Anything that will actually help us catch them, I mean?"

"No." Kat echoed his sigh. "I had one of my assistants get me some material on them. I don't suppose it will help to know that their scientific name is *mephitis mephitis*."

"I seriously doubt it. Unless it's a code for telling us how to nail one."

"Not even close. *Mephitis* means foul or evil smelling. Saying it twice means double the stink."

He looked at her, stunned. "And that's all you were armed with to come out here?"

Kat smiled and lifted her shoulders in a small shrug. "Hey, you take what you can get in this field. So, what do you know about them?"

"Enough to run when they get mad," he said dryly.

"I'm impressed." She grinned at his wry look. "How can you tell?"

"When to run?"

"When they're mad."

"Sweetheart, you can't miss it."

"Don't you believe it. You can miss anything if you don't know what to expect." She pulled out a notepad and a pencil. "Go on, talk."

"Okay, when skunks are mad, they— What are you doing, taking notes?"

"Don't get a big head, Ryder. We scientific types do this

all the time." She nudged him in the ribs with her elbow. "Come on, give."

"They stamp their front feet. What?" He met her frown with an innocent smile. *"What?"*

"Are you making this up? Is this a 'let's have fun with a tenderfoot' day?"

Mac raised his hand as if taking a vow. "Swear to God. Come on, Doc. If you're going to give me grief over a little thing like that, how are you going to act when I tell you the rest?"

"You mean there's more? As idiotic as that?"

"Worse." His smile broadened to a grin when she rolled her eyes. "Okay, they stamp their front feet again and make a hissing or chattering noise with their teeth. You getting all this?" He peered at the notepad until she heaved a sigh and looked up, narrowing her eyes.

"And then?" she asked between clenched teeth.

"If you haven't gotten the message and taken off by that time, they lift their tails high over their backs. Then they twist their bodies in a U-shape, so both their faces and rears are pointed at you, and they let loose."

Kat studied her notes, then looked up with a blink. "That doesn't sound too bad."

"Honey, have you ever smelled fresh skunk?"

She shook her head. "Uh-uh."

"I can tell you from firsthand experience, you don't want to. Besides, it's not just the smell. It's a fluid, and they can squirt up to about ten feet with good aim. They aim for your eyes and if the stuff hits dead-on, it can temporarily blind you and burn your skin."

"Good grief."

"Yeah. They're nothing to mess with."

"And that's exactly why we're here—to mess with them." Kat tucked the notepad and pencil back in her pocket. "This is a little more complicated than I thought it would be.'' After a long moment she pulled them back out again. ''Look, I know I'm out of my element here. My expertise is in the lab, after someone else has brought me blood samples that have been DNA tested.... So what else do you know? Anything about their eating habits? Anything that will help us find them? Faster?'' she added with asperity. ''Sitting on a dead log isn't exactly my idea of conducting a great skunk hunt.''

Mac gave her a patient look. ''Skunks will eat almost anything edible. In the summer, when there are insects and small animals up the kazoo, that's what they eat. Grasshoppers, crickets, birds eggs, chipmunks, rabbits—you name it, they'll eat it.

''In the fall and winter they mainly eat plants—bulbs, roots, flowers, whatever. They sometimes look under logs. Got that down?'' he asked, squinting over her shoulder. ''Logs, for grubs. Which is why we're sitting on a dead log surrounded by a lot of plants. Of course, we could go hiking along the roads, if you'd prefer. At this time of the year they sometimes hunt the roads for snakes, turtles and almost anything killed by cars.''

''Okay.'' Kat closed the notepad with an irritated snap. ''I apologize. You know what you're doing, and I don't. But would it hurt to explain a little of this along the way? That way, I wouldn't be working on an ulcer thinking that we're wasting—''

''Shh.'' Mac's hand closed around her arm. ''Listen.''

Kat felt her pulse jump at his whispered order. She tilted her head and several seconds later heard a slow, heavy movement through the tall grass. Crossing her fingers, she found herself torn. She devoutly hoped it was a skunk. Even more intensely, she wanted it *not* to be a grizzly. With a bear, the dart gun that had just appeared in Mac's hand would have about as much impact as a peashooter against an elephant.

"There's one thing I forgot to ask you," Mac murmured, his gaze focused on the undulating grass.

"What?" It was still too dark to see much, but she peered around nervously anyway. *"What?"*

"How fast does this thing work?"

Kat blinked. "I don't know. I guess as fast as you can pull the trigger."

Mac closed his eyes. When he opened them, Kat was looking up at him, a disconcerted expression on her face. "Oh. Sorry. You mean—"

"Yeah. How quickly will the tranquilizer take effect?"

"I don't know." She shook her head. "I never thought to ask. But I *do* know John, and he's a very fastidious man. He wouldn't underestimate the amount and take a chance on being squirted with that stuff."

"I hope to hell you're right."

"Me, too."

"I guess it'll work as long as we catch our striped friends before they know we're around."

"You mean, before they get their tails up?"

"Exactly." He held up a hand in a warning gesture then grinned. "Okay, Tonto," he whispered, gently squeezing her thigh. "Here he comes."

Several yards away a bush swayed. When it bounced back into place, its drying leaves jiggled and rasped. The skunk waddled out from behind its protective cover, stopping to turn over a large stone and investigate its moist underside.

Kat barely had time to admire the beautiful, bushy, black-and-white tail before Mac raised the dart gun and squeezed the trigger. The slight hissing sound came from the gun, not the skunk, she realized an instant later when the animal slowly sank back on its haunches then toppled over.

Reaching into the small case beside her, Kat withdrew a

pair of plastic gloves and pulled them on. Just as she started to slide off the tree, a second skunk ambled out from behind the bush. She felt Mac stiffen then reach in his coat pocket. He replaced the cartridge then slowly took aim.

The second one slumped in its tracks just as a third skunk worked its way through the tall grass.

"What the hell is this, a convention?" Mac breathed, reaching into his pocket again. He dealt with the third one as efficiently as he had the first two then scanned the area for any more before turning to Kat. "Come on, Doc, we'd better hustle." She jumped down and grabbed the case while he slid another cartridge in the gun. "How long do we have before they start stirring?"

"Less than five minutes," she murmured, kneeling by the first skunk. "We like to get animals back on their feet as soon as possible."

"What can I do to help? I don't think your buddies were expecting a mass production scene here."

"You've done your share." She opened the case and pulled out a self-sealing plastic bag. "Just keep a lookout for any more of these critters while I do this."

She was efficient, Mac noted. All business, and fast. The city girl was in her element for the moment. He hunkered down on his heels beside her, watching as she slid the needle in and withdrew a small amount of blood.

Sometime earlier, Kat had organized her supplies. Each plastic bag contained a syringe, a small, numbered ear tag and a labeled vial for the blood. She had already written the number of the tag on the vial, so now all she had to do was attach the ear tag, seal the syringe in the bag and move on to the next one. The blood could be transferred to the vial when they got back to camp.

"Here." She tossed him a small bottle with a pump action lid. "It's food coloring. Spray a bit on the tail, so we'll know which ones we've done." She grabbed another plastic bag and moved on to the next skunk.

"Fast work, Doc." It had taken her less than a minute, closer to forty seconds.

"Yeah. Fear's a great motivator. Now that I know just how nasty our friends here can get, I want to be out of squirting distance if another one comes strolling down the pike." She sealed the third bag and stood up. "All done. Now we can watch them from a safe distance and make sure they're okay. It's getting a little lighter, so that will help."

Later, back at camp, Mac asked, "What would you have done if one of them hadn't gotten up?"

Kat wrinkled her nose and looked up from the small ice chest containing the blood samples. "I don't even want to think about it. I would've had to go back and try to help it."

"Even if you ran the risk of being sprayed by the others?"

She nodded. "Even then."

And that, Mac reflected, was that. End of discussion. She would go back because it was her job. He watched her jot a note in a logbook, impatiently brushing her hair away from her face, and knew it was more than that. She would go back because that was the way she was made. She was here to save the world, not leave a string of maimed or dead animals trailing behind her.

Kat looked up and caught him staring at her. "What? You have a question, cowboy?"

"Yeah, now that you mention it." He sauntered over to the table and sat across from her, propping his elbows on the table. "Why was last night a first for you?"

"Good grief." She narrowed her eyes to slits. When he smiled, she wanted to smack him. "Look, Mac, I don't know how things are done in Wyoming, but where I come from people don't sit around at ten in the morning talking about things like this.''

"Really?" He glanced at his watch. "Okay, what's a good time?"

She jumped up and made a production of tucking her logbook in her briefcase. "There isn't one. The subject is closed."

Leaning back in his chair, Mac gave her a bland look. "You have to admit, it's an interesting one. Here you are, what—thirty, thirty-one, and you've never had a—"

"Twenty-nine," she said through gritted teeth. "And it's none of your business what I have or haven't had."

"Sure it is." His eyes were wide and earnest, and his smile maddened her. "How am I going to seduce you, if we have this major problem here."

Kat's flat gaze was hot enough to singe his hair. "*We* don't have a problem. *We* don't have anything."

"Wrong, Doc. We're in this thing together. All the way."

She heaved a sigh that made him grin. "Mac, I hate to be the one to break this to you, but you are not irresistible. I have no intention of going to bed with you. I told you that right from the start."

"That's okay. I have intentions enough for both of us."

And he did. He had felt a jolt to his senses the first time he saw her, wet and bedraggled as she was, and nothing since then had changed. His first sight of her in Claude's jeans had almost knocked him to his knees. He'd figured it couldn't get much better—but that was before he'd rescued her luggage from the car.

Clad in her own conservative pleated slacks and tailored silk shirts, Kat was cool, casual and pure class. She made his hands sweat and his heart pound. He had spent two days memorizing every curve and hollow revealed in the

tight jeans, and he knew exactly what was being covered
by her elegant, flowing outfits.

But there were other things that made his pulse stutter.
The tenderness in her eyes when she was with Davy. Her
choked laughter when Claude told her a whopper. Her sparkle when she talked about her work. Her ruffled look when
she caught him watching her. And the unconscious hunger
in her eyes when she turned her gaze on him.

He hadn't wanted things to turn out this way, he reflected
moodily, watching her pace from the table to the tent. He
had put his feelings in cold storage a long time ago and
didn't want them thawed out. His plan had been straightforward enough.

Sex. Hot sex with a woman he liked. And when it was
over, she would leave. They'd both have good memories
and no regrets. Simple. Clean. Temporary.

Yeah, that's the way it was supposed to be, but somewhere along the way the game plan had changed. Kat had
worked her way under his skin. She touched him as no
woman had in years. And he wanted her. Hell, he got
aroused every time he thought of her. But now it wasn't
enough just to have a soft, curvy woman in his arms. He
wanted Kat, with her heart-stopping uncertainties, her quick
fuse, her absorbed interest in her work, which could have
been dull but was so damn sexy when she talked about it
that it tied him up in knots.

On the other hand, he knew for certain that he wouldn't
bring another city woman full of innocence and laughter to
the ranch. He had made that mistake once and lived with
enough grief and guilt to last a lifetime. Sure, their marriage
had already developed a few cracks, but his carelessness
had ended it before they could be filled in. His negligence
had robbed their baby of his mother.

It had been his responsibility to take care of his wife,
and he had failed. He had assumed too much, had forgotten

how little she knew of life outside the city. He had taught her how to ride, but nothing at all about the unforgiving weather. As a result, she hadn't had a hope in hell of protecting herself when the unexpected storm caught her miles from the house.

His fault.

He lived with the knowledge, and the only way he could survive was to know it would never happen again. If he married again, it would be to a local woman, someone who knew ranches and understood all the risks involved.

But none of that changed his bargain with Kat, he reflected, following her with his gaze. This wasn't a marriage; it was an affair between two consenting adults. Assuming he could get her to agree. With only one slight difference, he brooded. When it was over, it wouldn't be as clean or easy as he'd thought. He would miss her, damnably—and have a mountain of regrets for what could never be.

Kat muttered something, and he turned to watch her stomp into the tent. At this rate, she'd have a rut in the ground before lunch, he thought idly, wondering what she'd be wearing when she came out. She changed clothes every couple of hours, as the temperature rose and fell, and every outfit seemed designed to drive him crazy.

When she emerged a few minutes later wearing pink shorts and a matching tank top, Mac groaned.

Kat looked up, swift concern in her eyes. "What's the matter?"

"You. Those clothes." His gesture took in the abbreviated outfit.

Baffled, she gazed at him for a long moment. Then realization flickered in her eyes—followed by amusement. "Get a grip, cowboy. If a simple pair of shorts can do this to you, you're in a bad way."

"I am," he said promptly. "A terrible way. After last night—"

"Forget last night." Kat's frown was broken by a yawn that caught her by surprise. "Sorry."

"Tired?" Mac asked, scooting a chair back with a booted foot and waving her toward it.

She nodded and sat down. "Wiped out. That bear put me on an adrenaline overload, and I think I've crashed." She carefully avoided mentioning anything that followed the grizzly's visit.

"Why don't you take a nap?"

"I thought about it, but the tent's too hot."

"Yeah, it usually is once the sun comes out. That's why I brought a hammock."

Kat's eyes brightened. "A hammock?"

"Yep. One of those wide ones, on a metal frame."

"Umm." She made a purring sound in her throat. "Sounds like heaven."

Mac shrugged. "Depends."

Kat blinked at him. "On what?"

"On how much you want it. You take the hammock, you get me along with it."

Studying his expression, Kat sighed. Determination and amusement lightened his dark eyes, and she knew he meant every word. Stubborn, she reflected. Mule stubborn.

Too tired to give him the argument he obviously wanted, she gave him a brief nod. "Haul it out, cowboy. But remember, it's not a playpen. We're sleeping. Nothing else. Sleeping, got it?"

"Got it, Doc." He turned away, grinning. "Got it."

Eight

Three days later Mac shouldered open the kitchen door. "Davy? Claude?"

Kat dumped the small ice chest on the table and leaned over to pick up the note held down by the sugar bowl. "They're gone," she told him, frowning over Claude's cramped writing. "The school in Denver called, so they hopped a plane."

She jumped when Mac slid an arm around her waist and read over her shoulder. "They left yesterday," she murmured, locking her knees so she wouldn't slump against him. "Staying at my condo...he says they might be gone a week."

Mac tightened his arm a fraction before he let her go and moved over to the sink. "That's what I told him to do. No sense in waiting for us to come back. I want to get this damn testing over with."

Kat followed him, wanting to relieve the sudden tension

humming through him, not certain she knew how. "You don't have to worry about Davy," she said matter-of-factly. "The counselors are wonderful."

"Yeah. I suppose." He rolled his shoulders and gave a bone-popping stretch.

"Come here." Tugging at his sleeve, Kat led him to a chair. "Sit." He sat, stiffening when she rested her palms against his neck. "Let Doctor Wainwright work some of the kinks out of your neck while you worry."

"I'm not worried."

"Liar." She dug her thumbs in and smiled when he jerked. "You're allowed. Good daddies do things like that. It's okay."

"I don't want Davy upset. Or scared."

"He won't be." She ground the heel of her hand against a tight muscle. "I promise."

"You sound awful sure about it," Mac muttered, wincing.

"I am. I hung around when Cody was there. There's no schoolroom atmosphere, no stress. They make a game out of everything. I can guarantee that right now Davy is having the time of his young life. Look at it this way," she said brightly, hoping to distract him. "He isn't out chasing skunks, and he won't be going back in a few days to chase some more."

"I should be with him."

Kat sighed. "Hey, I was there when you talked with Davy, remember? Your son has a rare understanding of responsibility. He's the one that told you Claude should go with him so you could keep an eye on things around here."

"I know." He swore in frustration. "He worries like a little old man."

"Gee, I wonder where he picked that up." Kat slipped her arms around his neck and gave him a quick hug, then stepped back before he could turn around. "I'm going upstairs to take a bath. After three days of washing in an icy stream, I'm a desperate woman. My big plan for the next couple of hours is to wallow in hot water, so I'll see you when I see you.''

She stopped in the doorway and looked back at the clock. ''Davy and Claude should be back at my condo pretty soon. Why don't you give them a call?''

Before he could reply, she turned and headed down the hall. Time, she thought, trotting up the stairs. That's what she needed. And space.

Spending three days in the wilderness would have been a challenge just in itself. Dealing with annoyed skunks and hungry grizzlies had added a new dimension to her life—fear bordering on outright terror.

But spending three days in close quarters with a sexy man bent on seduction had been even more unnerving—for more than one reason. She was accustomed to working in her own lab, alone. Living alone. While she wouldn't exactly call herself a hermit, she did need a certain amount of time for herself.

Living with Mac in a tent that was mostly mattress had made her feel slightly claustrophobic. Waking in the middle of the night to hear a man breathing next to her—even if he was zipped in his own sleeping bag—had been disconcerting. Spending every waking hour with him, feeling his gaze move over her, was downright nerve-racking.

And that wasn't even counting the times she'd spent sleeping in his arms in the swaying hammock. They had been among the best, and the worst.

After Kat turned the faucets and poured in some bath oil, she stood, watching the steamy water pound into the tub and remembering. After that first night, when Mac had taken her to heights she'd never dreamed of, then soothed and held her until she'd slept, he had backed off. He hadn't rushed her.

He had been more subtle than that. When she'd met his gaze, it had made promises. Silently. Lavishly. His voice had held an invitation. His casual touches had jolted and echoed through her body.

And somehow, during those three days, she had fallen in love.

Kat eased into the fragrant water and leaned back, gazing at the ceiling. In love. The idea still stunned her.

It wasn't at all the way she had thought it would be, she reflected, flipping away a mound of foam drifting toward her chin. Years earlier, she had visualized love as a romantic miracle of candlelight, soft words and music. And as time passed, despite the pragmatic nature of her work and a definite lack of romance in her life, she had unconsciously continued to nurture the fantasy. Had hoped as much as believed that it actually existed.

And then she'd met a furious rancher who swore and called her names. A man who didn't want her around but still ripped open his coat to share his body heat. A man who wanted to keep his painful memories locked away but faced them every time he looked at her. And she had learned that love was so much more—tougher, grittier— than she'd ever dreamed.

Love was a hard man with gentle hands...and eyes that grew tender when he looked at his young son. Love was a man who sacrificed his future because he couldn't forgive himself for the past. And love was a man who hungered but would take only what was offered.

Love was a woman who was...needy. For a particular man. It was an ache that clawed at her. It was the exultation she felt when she saw desire in his eyes and felt it burn her body. It was a seesaw from despair to joy; it was terror at the unknown.

It was scary, she concluded, shaking her head at the understatement. Especially for a woman whose life's work required endless speculation about the future. In this case, Kat reflected, the future wasn't rosy. In fact, there *was* no future.

Because in this instance, permanence wasn't an issue. Mac wanted her all right—on a temporary basis. Oh, he made no secret of how *much* he wanted her, but that wasn't the point. Because, she suspected, what he wanted was simply a woman. A woman—not specifically Dr. Kathryn Wainwright. Or Kat. Or even Doc.

Any woman would do.

"Any woman," she murmured, feeling her heart break a little.

And for that reason they had stayed in separate sleeping bags. For that reason she hadn't said yes to the question he silently asked every time he looked at her. She had resisted the promise of glory for fear of pain.

When Kat finally swung open the bathroom door, wearing a midnight blue towel like a sarong, another as a turban, she stopped as if she had run into a glass wall.

Mac was leaning in the doorway directly across from her. He looked like he'd been there a long time. His hair was still damp from the shower, and he hadn't bothered with many clothes.

Jeans. That was it. A low-riding pair of jeans and a lot of skin. And he was waiting. For her.

Massive shoulders honed by hard physical labor. Broad chest sprinkled with dark hair that tapered at his narrow waist and disappeared inside his jeans. Sculpted muscles moving fluidly beneath tan skin. The expression in his dark eyes that said he was tired of waiting.

Her thoughts came in short bursts while her gaze swept over him in mingled apprehension and delight. He was gorgeous. A montage of masculine beauty. She almost smiled, thinking how he would hate the description.

Kat jolted when he shouldered away from the wall, felt her eyes widen when he stopped in front of her. She caught his scent, soap and pure male, and clutched the doorjamb to steady herself. His heat surrounded her, and she wanted nothing more than to be a part of it, be a part of him.

Mac framed her face with his hands, using the pressure of his thumbs to tilt her face.

"Mac?" Her voice shook and she cleared her throat to try again.

"Shh." He bent his head to lightly brush her lips with his. Her shiver jolted him, set his pulse racing.

Kat ran her tongue along her lower lip, tasting him, tasting heat and hunger. She moved closer, drawn to him as if pulled by invisible wires.

"Kat?" His voice was rough with wanting. Needing. He slid the turban off her head so he could brush his fingertips over her hair.

She knew what he was asking and suddenly the answer was there, right along with a sizzling arrow to her belly. She wanted him, and she had worried about the future long enough. Besides, she believed in him, in herself, and in what they could be.

Oh, sure, the fear was still there. But so was hope. And exhilaration. She was taking a big risk, but whatever happened, it would be worth it.

"Yes." She saw the flicker of surprise in his eyes turn to heat and intent.

Mac's hands tightened, framing her face. Kat's lips moved, and he tried to hear her over the roar in his head. "Yes?"

"Yes." She smiled, and he forgot everything except how much he wanted her. Needed her.

"Now?" He took a deep breath, giving her one last chance.

Kat closed her eyes, not in thought, just wallowing in

sensations as she nuzzled her cheek against his shoulder. She didn't know if he had tugged her closer or if she'd made the move herself. She *did* know that after three days of thinking and worrying, she was exactly where she wanted to be—pressed against Mac's hot, hard body and the undeniable evidence that he felt the same way she did.

She smiled and lifted her face. "Now."

Mac scooped her up and carried her to his room in a jumble of stark need, confusion and relief. He angled her through the door, no longer embarrassed about the glowing candles he had placed around the room before he went to get her. It had been a spontaneous gesture, something he had never done before. *A first,* he reflected as he dropped to the wide mattress, rolling to one side to keep his weight off her.

He didn't know why she'd finally said yes any more than he understood why she'd kept him at arm's length for the past three days.

He didn't really care.

She was in his arms, willing and hungry. That was the only thing that mattered.

Willing? he wondered, as her arms slid around his neck and she melted against him. Hell no, she was more than that. Much more, he thought exultantly as her fingers skimmed down his chest and headed for the waistband of his jeans.

"Doc?"

"Umm?"

"You're asking for trouble."

"Then I guess I'm in the right place." She gave him a teasing glance that knocked the breath out of him.

"Yeah." His fingers worked the knot of dark fabric at her breast, brushing against her silky skin as they moved. "You got that right."

Her scrubbed look set his heart drumming. One part of

his mind warned him he was in deep water while another part whispered that she smelled like sin, felt like silk.

When he unraveled the knot, the towel began slipping, an inch at a time. This time they weren't in a dark tent. This time, when he stroked the tip of her breast with his thumb he could see as well as feel it form a hard bead.

Her hair, already drying, slid forward when she restlessly moved her shoulders, tangling around his fingers.

"You're beautiful, Doc." He felt her surprise, her sigh, the shake of her head.

"No. Not beautiful. But thank you."

Mac leaned back, braced on his forearm, and looked. Gazed until her eyes flickered and her face pinkened. "You're right," he said finally. "You're not." He stroked a gentle finger along her jaw. "More like mud ugly."

He grinned when she narrowed her eyes. "But I have this thing about ugly women," he murmured, dropping a kiss at the corner of her eye. "I can't resist them."

He didn't stop there. His mouth trailed kisses down her throat, his lips curving when her pulse revved, then slowed down at the curve of her breasts. Slowed down but didn't stop.

The towel was still sliding, and it was doing such a good job on its own, Mac decided not to help it along. The decision was based on anticipation as much as sheer delight. Each time the fabric slipped another inch, his heart hitched and almost stopped. As each new curve and hollow was revealed, it jump-started again.

The last of the toweling tumbled to the bed, framing her golden body with vibrant color. He was reminded of paintings in museums, nudes with luscious skin reclining on swaths of fabric. As he skimmed a hand down her waist, let it rest on her hip, his eyes narrowed with fierce possession.

The stab of emotion stunned him. He didn't consider

himself a territorial man. Or hadn't. But this was different. *Kat* was different. The image of her lying on his bed, eyes clouded with passion and dreams, was not for museums and multitudes. It was for him. Only him.

Kat shifted restlessly beneath his gaze, wondering how the expression in Mac's eyes could shift so quickly, could move from teasing to heat to dark desire within just seconds. How it could build such an aching emptiness in her. How it could make her so desperate for the touch of his body against hers.

But it did, and she couldn't wait any longer.

"Mac?"

"Umm?" He was using his thumb to trace a line down the center of her body and sounded preoccupied.

"Come here." She shivered when his fingers touched her belly.

"Are we in a hurry here, Doc?"

Kat slid her hands across his shoulders and laced her fingers at his nape. "I am."

"Not me." He dropped a kiss on one breast, watched her beading nipple with approval then moved to the other one. "We've got all night. All the blessed night."

And he meant to cover every square inch of her body before it was over. First with his hands, then his mouth. And then? Maybe he'd just start all over again.

The other night in the tent, he knew Kat had been shocked to the marrow by her response to him. He had been thrilled beyond words. He wanted her to feel that wild storm again and again, until she knew for certain it wasn't a fluke. Until she believed that whatever had been missing in her life wasn't because of a lack in her.

A quick shudder shot through Kat when his fingers slid into the dark hair at the apex of her thighs, and she arched, pushing against his hand, when he touched the softness of her femininity.

"Mac."

He took a deep breath and let it out slowly. Her whisper, husky with need, rampant with yearning, could be packaged and sold for bait, he thought, fighting a slap of urgency that tore through him. It could snare every man within a hundred miles. Make them walk willingly into a trap, knowing the door would slam shut behind them. And they wouldn't give a damn—not as long as she was in there with them.

Murmuring a surprised protest, Kat twisted away and rolled to her knees, facing him. "Oh, no you don't, cowboy. Not tonight." Her breath came in spurts, and she held up a warning hand. "You're not going to drive me crazy and then tell me to go to sleep, the way you did the other night."

She shook her head and swiped impatiently at the hair that fanned across her face. "Wherever we go tonight, we go together."

Temper snapping in her eyes, she settled fisted hands on her hips. "Got that, cowboy? *Together.*"

With a rush that made Kat blink, Mac sat up and swung around until they were knee to knee. His gaze locked with hers and he wanted to shake her. She was pushing him, lousing up his plans, but she was magnificent. A young goddess, buck naked, raising hell. Testing, maybe a tad uncertain, but determined, and beginning to enjoy herself.

"Okay." His bland voice was a direct contrast to the heat in his eyes. "You've got my attention. What else do you want."

"You." The single word was breathless, but she wasn't backing down.

Mac lifted his shoulders in a shrug and grinned. "Then come and get me."

For one long, endless second, he thought Kat was going to lose her nerve. Instead she launched herself at him like a missile, knocking him flat. A second later she was perched on his thighs, straddling him.

Her hands were all over him, leaving a trail of fire as they moved, stroking, kneading, lingering. They settled at his waist, tugging to open his jeans. Mac clenched his teeth, swearing silently as she fumbled, but he did nothing to ease the torment.

"There." The single word, uttered when the button popped open, was a soft, satisfied sound.

Mac sucked in his breath when she tugged at the zipper. The goddess was impatient, determined, he thought, torn between tender amusement and wild, heart-pounding antici-pation. She was taking this at top speed, a far cry from the leisurely pace he had planned.

Slowing down, she eased the zipper over the strained jeans. Her eyes widened when she saw he had nothing on beneath them except...himself.

The look did it for Mac. No man could have resisted the wide-eyed wonder of it. He sure as hell couldn't.

"Hold that thought," he gritted. Clamping his hands at her waist, he lifted and tumbled her to the bed beside him. While she drew in a breath of protest, he tore off his pants and tossed them aside. Then before she could utter the words trembling on her lips, he lifted her again, settling her back on his thighs.

"Now, where were we?" he drawled.

She had an excellent memory. Mac stiffened, his heart pounding, as her hands skimmed over his chest, following the trail of hair arrowing down his belly.

And the leisurely seduction he had planned became a summer storm, all lightning and heat.

The touch of Kat's fingers brushing, cupping, wiped all the good intentions from his mind. There was no time to explore, to let his fingertips slide over her silky skin in long, intimate strokes.

He rolled to his side, taking her with him, touching his mouth to her breast, then down, to her belly, her thighs, her long, gorgeous legs.

"Mac!" Kat's eyes were drenched with need. She trembled in his arms, her breathing fast and hard. "Now."

"Soon," he promised huskily.

"Now." She tugged at his shoulders.

"Right." Promising himself it would be different, slower, the next time, he reached for a small packet on the table. He tore it open with shaking hands and eased back for a second, dropping another steamy kiss on her mouth.

When he slid into her, her breath caught and she melted against him. They moved together, and Kat cried out his name, over and over, until her voice shattered and she clung to him as if she'd never let him go. Her inner muscles tugged at him, drawing him deeper inside her. Mac linked his fingers with hers, slid her hands over her head, and felt his heart swell at the tremor that shook her body. Her name was on his lips when he reached the height of his passion.

It was dawn when Kat opened her eyes. Mac lay with his lips pressed against her throat, his breathing deep and even. Thinking he was asleep, she turned her face and kissed his shoulder.

She had been right, she thought lazily, running her fingers through his hair. With Mac, making love had been everything she'd dreamed it could be because Mac had touched her like no other man ever had.

She smiled, lazily content, wondering about the candles. Even though they didn't seem quite his style, they had glowed softly, mellowing the stark simplicity of the masculine room. The soft words had been hot, erotic, and the music had been the dance of their bodies. And the music had played on and on, she recalled with another smile, each time he had reached for her during the night.

Mac lifted his head and covered her mouth in a lingering kiss before he braced himself to move. "I'm too heavy for you."

"No." Her arms tightened around him, holding him where he was. "Don't leave."

"I didn't say I was going. Just...moving." He turned, taking Kat with him as he reversed positions. "That better?"

"It's...nice," she said sedately, nuzzling her cheek against his.

"Damned straight."

He sounded sinfully complacent, she decided, turning to plant a kiss on his jaw. As well as seductive and downright sexy.

"You okay?" He shaped her bottom with his large hand and squeezed gently to emphasize the question.

Kat nodded. "I'm wonderful. Maybe even spectacular."

"You got that right. No maybe about it." He studied her pensive expression. "What's the matter?"

"Nothing."

"Then what are you thinking?"

"That no man has ever wanted me the way you did last night." She folded her hands on his chest and rested her chin on them. "It was wonderful." Frightening, too. But more wonderful than scary.

Mac ran his hand down her arm. He was touched. Her solemn expression said more than her words, and he knew she had just given him a part of herself.

He framed her face with his hands, wanting to ask the question that was haunting him. He knew the answer already, but he wanted to hear the words from her.

Kat tilted her head. "What?"

"Was this a first for you, too?"

"Yeah." She grinned. "I've never jumped a man before."

"You shouldn't have to." He nudged her. "It's a serious question, Doc."

"Okay." She sighed. "Yeah, it was. Before, I just...went through the motions. I didn't know it could be like this."

Mac shook his head. "It sounds to me like Colorado has more than its share of stupid men."

"It's not their fault." Automatically she rose to their defense.

Anger jolted him. "Well, it's sure as hell not yours."

"You sound awfully sure about that."

Mac smoothed his hand down her back, stopping at the curve of her bottom. "Lady, we've shared this bed all night, and I can give you a written guarantee."

Kat's blinding smile was his reward. "Thanks. I'll remember that." Her hands dropped to his shoulders when he tensed. "What's the matter?"

"Nothing." He tightened his arms around her and turned. "I'm just getting us comfortable to make love again."

"Again?" She looked up at him, astounded. "Mac, you can't possibly..." She broke off, trembling, as she felt him harden beside her.

"You were saying?"

"Not a thing." Kat wrapped her arms and legs around him, clinging, feeling the beat of his heart speeding against hers. "Not a thing."

Nine

"**I** thought you were going to take a nap."

Mac's large hands rested on Kat's shoulders, gently massaging. She was wearing shorts and a tank top to celebrate another day of warmth and sunshine, and her skin felt like warm honey. He dropped a kiss in her hair and glanced at the busy computer screen before her. They were in his office, at the long table he'd set up for Davy's new equipment.

"You weren't there." She lifted a hand from the keyboard to touch his. "I couldn't settle down."

The simple words, the touch, the darting smile, set his pulse drumming, and he wanted more than anything to pick her up and haul her up to the bedroom. Or to the sofa right next to the computer. Anywhere where he could hold her. He settled for touching her cheek and hearing the hitch in her breath.

No one had ever turned his life upside down the way

Kat had done in just a few days, and he moved through the hours with just one thought. He wanted her. As he had never wanted before. Had never known he could want. It left a hole of need in him that a horse could walk through. A hole that only Kat could fill.

Mac touched her cheek again knowing it wasn't the promise of coffee that had brought him in from the barn. Nor lunch. Nor any of the other excuses that had turned his feet toward the house. He wanted Kat. Needed her. It was that simple. And that complicated. She was as vital to him as the sun and the wind and the water that filled his wells.

They had been at the house for two days, brought back temporarily to tend to business—his to see that the horses were being shifted to pastures nearer the house, and hers to ship the first batch of blood samples and complete the notes she had taken. And, whether she would admit it or not, Kat had needed a break from the great outdoors.

The days had been busy, with each of them tending to necessities. The nights had been...turbulent, needy, sweet and wild, and everything in between.

"Are you hungry?" Rattled by his nearness, Kat tossed the question out as she rested her hands on the keyboard and wondered if she would ever see that expression in his eyes without shivering. The utter concentration in his gaze was enough to rattle any woman. Especially one who had spent the last two nights in his arms and the following days trying to be sensible.

As questions went, it was fairly safe, she reflected wryly, blinking to cut off the contact—even for a few seconds. He knew by now that if he said yes, the best he'd get out of her was a tuna sandwich. Or peanut butter and jelly. The deal they'd made the first night of camping still stood—he cooked and she handled the cleanup. It was safer that way, for both of them.

Mac tipped his hat back an inch. "Tuna?" he asked cautiously.

She nodded. "Or worse."

"I'll pass for now." Or until hunger drove him into the pantry to snitch a bag of chips. "Actually, there's something in the barn I want to show you."

"Mac." She gave him a patient look. "I've been there, remember? I've seen what's in the barn. Horses. Big horses with big teeth and bigger hooves."

"And you think they don't like you." He tried and failed to hide his grin.

"I *know* they don't. Not the way they stick their heads out of the stalls and curl their lips at me."

"They're just being friendly. And curious." He took a moment's pleasure by running a hand down the long thick braid that nestled between her shoulders. She had fixed it that way the first day in camp, saying it was practical. He liked it for an entirely different reason—it made her look touchable, not a bit like a pragmatic doctor. It also gave her a look of wide-eyed anticipation that was irresistible.

"That's not the way to begin a lasting friendship," she said dryly. "At least, not in my books."

Mac laughed. He couldn't help it. She was cute when she was nervous. And she was, when she thought about the barn, as nervous as she was serious.

"Now dogs I understand," she added, shivering when his hand slid up to her nape. "They wag their tails and lick you to death. And if they curl their lips and show their teeth, they're feeling very unfriendly. Ergo…"

"Ergo nothing." He reached for her hand and pulled her up beside him. "Horses aren't dogs. They're not planning to bite. They're not even thinking about it. Trust me."

She gave him a look loaded with suspicion. "I never trust anyone who says 'Trust me.'"

"So, do you have a few minutes?"

"No, not if this is all a devious plan to get me on a horse."

"Not today." He wrapped his arm around her shoulders and turned her toward the door. Incredible as it seemed, she really was tense around the horses, acting as if they were going to sneak up behind her and have her for supper. Not too bright for a genius, but that was her theory and she seemed to be sticking to it.

The trick, he'd decided, was to start her out with something small and work up to the real thing. Something nonthreatening.

"Haven't you ever been around horses?" he asked with genuine curiosity.

"Of course I have." Her chuckle disarmed him. "I even rode one. Once. When I was a kid. It threw me off and drooled all over me. I never went back for seconds, and I don't intend to now."

Kat hooked her thumb in his back pocket and let her hip bump companionably against his as they walked. "I'm not real crazy about cows, either," she reminded him.

"Cattle, Doc, cattle." He wondered fleetingly if she was trying to get at him or just forgetful. They'd been through this before. "You milk cows. How anyone with an IQ the size of yours can have so much trouble understanding a simple thing like that—"

"I don't sweat the small stuff." She waved an airy hand, the gesture taking in the yard and anything that didn't directly involve her work.

"Right." His ranch, all ninety thousand acres of it, plus another big chunk of leased land, wasn't exactly peanuts. He tightened his arm around her waist, thinking that even if she didn't know a side of beef from a milking machine she still looked damn good in the afternoon light. Of course, she looked just as tasty by the light of a campfire, by moonlight and candlelight. He knew that for a fact.

"So. What's in the barn?"

Mac grinned. It hadn't taken her long to buck for the bottom line. She had a habit of doing that, he'd noticed. It was as much a part of her makeup as the quick laughter and competence. The impatience and the serenity that overrode her agile mind.

"You're not answering," she muttered, narrowing her eyes. "So help me, if you've got something awful in there—"

He shoved back his hat a notch, his expression bland. "Kat, my *horses* are in there. Be reasonable."

"Sorry, I lost my grip for a second." Kat rolled her eyes. "Can't imagine what I was thinking."

As Mac opened the barn door, he slipped his hand to the small of her back and urged her inside. "It's in the back. Wait a minute, let me get the lights."

He hit the switch and led her to the rear of the structure. Kat walked beside him, jumping when a big brown horse stuck its head out of the stall and whickered.

"I think he's checking me out for his next snack," she muttered, moving closer to Mac.

He blew out his breath in a big sigh. "They aren't carnivorous."

She cast a suspicious glance at the huge animal. "Has anyone told him that?"

"Her."

"*Her?* Good grief, what are the babies like?"

He stopped, flipping the latch on the stall gate. "Take a look."

Kat took a cautious peek around the door. "Oh, Mac, look at her."

"Him," he said on a sigh.

"Him, then. Isn't he precious? Oh, come here, you cute thing." She dropped to her knees on the clean straw bedding and lured the leggy, young colt closer with soft words and gentle fingers.

She looked up, delight in her eyes. "How old is he?"

"A few months." Mac stepped into the stall and moved toward the back, out of their way. "He was born in late spring."

She turned back, running her hand down the colt's neck, whispering into his flickering ear. "You're a darling, that's what you are."

Sitting on a pile of straw in the corner, Mac grinned at the pair of them. Kat was all but cooing, her eyes tender as the colt bravely edged closer and nuzzled her cheek. Straightening his legs, Mac crossed his booted feet at the ankles and leaned back against the rough, wooden wall watching them.

Cute? he reflected. *Precious?* Kat was stroking the future of his horse-breeding program, the culmination of several years' work, and all she thought was *darling?* He took a piece of carrot from his shirt pocket and handed it to her.

"Here. Put it in your palm and keep your hand flat. Don't rush him. Champ will take it when he's ready."

She frowned at him, absently following his instructions. "Champ? That's the best you could come up with for this little guy? It makes him sound like a broken-down boxer."

"You'd probably like his registered name better, but it's a mouthful."

She jumped and forgot her lecture when the colt's velvety muzzle touched her hand. Laughing softly, she said, "Look, he's eating it."

"Yeah." Mac nodded, enjoying her pleasure. "And you still have your hand. Amazing."

"Cute, Ryder." Kat rubbed her damp palm on the side of her jeans. "Real cute. I suppose that was a lesson in—"
An anxious whicker, answered by a squeal from the colt,

interrupted her, and she raised inquiring brows. "What's going on?"

"A family discussion." Mac got to his feet. "The man-eater next door is his mama, and she's getting anxious. She wants him back in there with her." He gentled the colt and opened the stall. "Come on, fella, let's take you home." Kat followed, sticking close to Mac to watch the reunion.

The worried mother nuzzled her baby. When she was satisfied that he had survived his absence, she stuck her head over the stall door and snorted. Kat backed up nervously, stopping when she ran into Mac.

"Nice kid you have, lady," she said feebly.

When Mac's arm tightened around her waist, Kat stilled, struggling to get air into her lungs. Her heart jumped when he pulled her back into the stall they had just vacated.

Would his touch always affect her this way? she wondered, sliding her hand over his. Would she feel boneless every time he looked at her? Would his hard body be the only one that ever felt like a perfect match?

Probably.

Kat turned in his arms and gazed up at him. His dark hair was rumpled beneath the straw hat, looking as if he had run his fingers through it as he worked. He smelled faintly of soap, heat and the clean sweat of a working man. And his eyes answered her question before she could ask.

He wanted her.

Here.

Now.

"Kat?" The word was a husky whisper, sharpened by hope and need.

She smiled and reached for the top button of his shirt. In a stable, she thought. On a bed of straw, and all I can do is nod yes. The where didn't matter, she realized, her fingers moving to the next button. It wasn't important.

Wherever Mac was, she was safe—and exactly where she wanted to be.

Somehow they were out of their clothes. Somewhere Mac found a blanket and spread it over the straw. When he lowered her onto it and followed her down, she opened her arms, welcoming him, wanting him.

Mac slid into her embrace, telling himself he would take it slow. He would show her how tender he could be. Romance, he promised himself. He'd give her romance.

He forgot his good intentions as soon as she wrapped her arms around him. His blood was too hot, his nerves too jangled, his need too great. If he didn't have her now, right now, he would shatter into hundreds of pieces—each one needy and hungry.

His mouth covered hers in a long, desperate kiss, and he tasted a hunger as deep as his. Not surrender. It would never be that, he realized hazily. Not with Kat. Not as she was now, luxuriating in her own femininity. Pleasure surged through him at the thought. He'd had some small part in her electrifying transformation. No, Kat would meet him, match him and try to outdistance him at every step.

When her hands restlessly traced his back, he felt an impatience that matched his own. He yanked the ribbon from her braid, then slowed down long enough to finger-comb her hair so he could fill his hands with the silky stuff.

Kat twisted against him, running her hands over his hard body as far as she could reach. Muscles bunched beneath her fingers, and his heart pounded against hers. She opened her mouth, tensing when his tongue sought and found hers.

More need. She tasted it, felt its dark spell, and the impact pushed her closer. Closer to him, closer to the tension tightening her body, to the shuddering release waiting for her.

Mac's hot mouth trailed down her neck, over the curve of her breasts and settled on a taut nipple with a groan of pleasure, tugging until she cried out, clutching at him. When he stilled, he felt her racing heart against his cheek. He drew in a long, hot breath and shifted lower, his lips skimming her ribs, drifted down across her belly.

Kat stiffened, her hands tearing at the blanket beneath her then moving to his hair. Tension bowed her body until she thought she would shatter. She parted her lips to tell him to stop, not to stop, but when his mouth touched her she cried out. It was an exultant sound of need fulfilled, of trust, of joy.

Mac reached out for his discarded pants, his heart almost stopping until his fingers settled on the foil band in his pocket. He tore it open, then in one swift movement, he moved up and joined his body to hers, heated flesh sliding against slick, hot flesh. Kat clutched at him, wrapping herself around him. She couldn't breathe, couldn't think.

Just feel.

Her nerve endings were a mass of jangled sensations, and she met each thrust of his body with wonder, feeling the shock, wanting more. Getting more until she thought she could take no more, until her cry met and matched Mac's, until he shuddered and rested his head beside hers.

She could get used to a barn, Kat reflected idly, shifting to a more comfortable position atop Mac. It wasn't bad. Actually, with the sweet smell of hay, the movements of horses safely locked in their own stalls, the steady beat of Mac's heart beneath her cheek, it was nice.

When his large hands moved from her waist to shape her bare hips, she knew he was awake. Stacking her hands on his chest, she propped her chin on them and looked down to meet his gaze. His dark eyes glimmered with satisfaction, and she smiled for no reason other than she felt like smiling.

She lazily moved a slim finger through a thatch of his springy dark chest hair. "I was just wondering."

Mac's brows rose. "What?"

"If I should cover my bare bottom."

"Why bother?" He moved his hands a bit. "I'm doing a good enough job."

"Not if we're going to have a horde of cowboys invading the place pretty soon."

He cocked his head. "Are we?"

"I don't know. That was more or less a question."

"No. We're not."

"You sure?"

"Positive. Most of them are out bringing some horses down from the higher elevations and won't be back for several days. The others have no reason to be here."

"Oh." She thought about that for a few seconds. "Mac?"

"Umm?"

"Why haven't you introduced me to any of them?"

He closed his eyes, knowing she felt him stiffen. Because of that, his reply was more succinct than usual. "They're busy."

Damn right they were. He was making sure of it, because however long Kat stayed on the ranch, it wouldn't be long enough. He was in no mood to share her time or attention. She was his for as long as she was here.

She was his.

He considered the words, knowing that would all change when she left. When her job was done, she would go. He would send her on her way.

Mac took a deep breath, acknowledging bleakly that he didn't want her finding another man. The thought made him feel murderous. Wondering about the men in her past wasn't much better. He remembered everything she had said about them; he just had a gut feeling that she'd left out a few details. It didn't make sense that a woman as sensual as Kat would have been content to live an almost nunlike existence.

"Doc?" He ran his hand up her back, tracing her spine with his fingers and deliberately putting aside thoughts of her leaving. They had one more trip ahead of them, more skunks to find. He wouldn't allow himself to think beyond that point.

"Hmm?"

"Tell me again about those blockheads in Denver." He took it as a good sign when she didn't tense up. She was smiling when he opened his eyes. "What?"

"You're interested in some really weird things." She shifted again, propping her elbows on his chest and cupping her chin in a raised palm. "It's an incredibly boring story. And the men aren't stupid," she added as an afterthought. "Some of then are charming, intelligent and very nice."

"So tell me this boring story," he prodded, admiring the view he had of her breasts.

"I was the one with the problem," she said finally, her eyes hazy with memories. "I think I told you that. There was nothing wrong with the boys or the men. They were average, normal. I wasn't. It was a genuine case of a fish out of water.

"I was a very young and naive seventeen when I entered college. I could have gone earlier, but my parents— wisely—wouldn't permit it. Academically I could handle myself with the best of them. Socially it was a different story. The boys, or men, were all several years and worlds of experience ahead of me. I just never caught up."

"Why not?"

"I think you know why." Her intelligent eyes took in his waiting expression. "That night in the tent, you showed that you understood."

"Humor me." He waggled his brows. "Tell me, anyway."

Kat sighed. "I missed the preliminaries, the innocent dates that provide experience and build confidence. When I finally started dating, I felt like everyone knew the rules except me. It was a miserable time. I finally went to bed with someone just to find out what all the fuss was about."

"And?" Mac held his breath. He didn't want her to say she'd been hurt—or that it had been fantastic. He didn't know what he wanted to hear.

Kat grinned reminiscently and Mac's stomach tightened. "I didn't find anything to fuss about."

He gave her bottom a light squeeze to conceal his relief. "Then what?"

Lifting her bare shoulders in a small shrug, she said lightly, "Scientific curiosity being what it is, I tried again. Several times over the years."

"How many years?"

"It doesn't matter." She gave him a flustered glance. "At any rate, I still didn't discover anything worth shouting over, so I quit trying. End of story."

"Kat—"

"Hey, I told you it was a boring story. Don't blame me if you don't like the ending." She tried to slip away but was stopped when his arm tightened around her waist.

"But that wasn't the end," he reminded her, holding her against him. "How long has it been since the last time you tried?"

"Last night, and it was very nice, thank you." She grinned down at him but avoided meeting his gaze.

"I'll make it easier," he said mildly. "How long has it been since you were with a man other than me?"

She gave him a quick scowl. "That's none of your business."

"I'm making it mine. How long?"

"You mean in bed?"

His arm tightened another notch. "Quit stalling."

"Almost three years," she muttered.

Rolling to his side, Mac took her with him. Supporting her head in the crook of his arm, he blinked down at her. "Three years?"

Narrowing her eyes to slits, she nodded. "Three. Years. Got it?" When he nodded, she blew out a huff of air. "It's no big deal, okay?"

Muscles flexed beneath her head as he shifted. "After what we've had here, you can say that?"

"I didn't know that before, did I?" she asked reasonably. "Look, it's like a guy who decides to try out for a sport and finds out he doesn't have a knack for it. So what does he do? If he's reasonably well-balanced, he doesn't pound his head against a stone wall for the rest of his life. He finds something else to do, like painting or photography."

"Photography," he echoed, studying her serene expression. "So what did you take up?"

"Gymnastics. I started as a kid, to burn off excess energy, and kept it up through high school and college. Other than that, work. I'm good at it," she said simply. "Before I was even out of school, Dan Matlock was hovering around with an offer to work for him." It had been a blatant case of courting the brightest of the bright, she remembered with no false modesty. The fact that he'd known her family for years had been a plus for both of them.

Mac stiffened. "Who's Dan Matlock?"

"A multimillionaire with a conscience, as well as an old family friend. He funded a few projects that my parents worked on. They're in biological science," she added in a quick aside. "Anyway, Dan made me an offer I couldn't refuse. He had pulled together some of the top brains in the country to work on ecological problems, and he wanted me to join them. The center is in Denver. As bait, he offered me my own lab and the autonomy to blaze my own path.''

Kat reached up to touch his cheek. ''And that's where I've been for the last five years. End of story.''

''And now you're out chasing skunks.'' Mac got to his feet and reached down to pull her up beside him. ''He must be proud.''

''As a matter of fact,'' she said loftily, catching the shirt Mac tossed her and pulling it over her head, ''he's fascinated by the idea. By the possibilities. He's very anxious to see the results of the DNA tests.''

She stopped talking as Mac stepped into his briefs. It was a shame to cover that beautiful body with clothes, she thought, watching him tug the jeans up long muscular legs sprinkled with crisp, dark hair and over narrow hips. He shrugged into his shirt, tucking it at the waist and buttoning his jeans. It was more than a shame, she decided as he pulled on his boots. It was a crime.

''How early will you be ready to leave in the morning?'' He buckled his belt and looked up, catching her staring. Grinning, he repeated the question. Damn, she made him feel good when she looked at him with those hungry blue eyes. She looked ready to take a chunk out of him.

''What?'' She blinked. ''Oh. Tomorrow. Anytime. I already have my stuff packed.'' She linked her fingers with his as they walked toward the door. ''Are we going back to the same place?''

''No. I think we milked the area dry. We got...how many samples there?''

''Fifteen.''

''A good amount for one location.'' Mac opened the door and waited until she stepped outside.

''Good, but not nearly enough. I'd like to have another thirty or forty.''

''How much time do you have?''

Kat took a steadying breath before she responded to the curt question. It was a point that both of them had avoided discussing—one that made her stomach knot just thinking about it. "Two more weeks."

His fingers clenched her shoulder until she almost cried out. "We'll make it," he said briefly, looking up to scan the blue sky. "As long as the weather holds out."

"Then we'll hold positive thoughts." She kept her voice airy in a deliberate attempt to lighten the suddenly charged atmosphere. "Let's go check the office and see if Davy's faxed us anything in the past few hours. I think it was definitely one of my better ideas to tell him how to work the gizmo when we talked the other night."

Ten

One week left.

Kat looked up from her logbook, where she had meticulously noted their current location, and gazed across the valley to the jagged mountains in the distance. The new site had much in common with the other three they'd stayed at, she reflected. There was a long swath of grass, resembling a wide, meandering ribbon of green, cutting through the timber. And water. Mac always found a place near a clear, running stream.

One week.

She had learned something about herself these last couple of weeks, Kat decided. She definitely wasn't hardy pioneer stock. Mother Nature had pulled out all the stops lately, offering daily thunderstorms, slippery mud to slog through, wet branches to wrestle with and other assorted annoyances. It had not been fun.

Her reaction wasn't prompted by ignorance. Not precisely. She could identify every tree in the area, both by its Latin and common name. Ditto with the plants. But that didn't mean she wanted to live among them. No, she had arrived at a momentous conclusion as she'd trudged through the gummy, dripping landscape. She would dedicate her life to saving the environment, do her best to clean up the messes that others inflicted on the land, but she would leave the wilderness to more adventurous souls.

If she had any choice in the matter, once this job was over, she would never again spend a night beneath the stars. Bear grunts, owl hoots and coyote cries had given her a permanent twitch. The amazing thing to her was that some people considered camping fun. Big-time fun.

Well, they could have her share. She would take her indoor bathroom, complete with tub, shower and quantities of hot water, any day. She would also take nature in smaller doses—like picnics.

One week.

Kat closed the book and automatically tucked it in her briefcase, firmly telling herself she was not nervous. She was in the center of nowhere, for heaven's sake. It was *supposed* to be quiet. There was nothing eerie about it at all. Of course, it would be nice to hear a couple of birds chirping. To hear anything.

Anything other than the sound of gunfire.

She got up and opened the tent flap, remembering the intent look on Mac's face less than an hour ago. He had been standing exactly where she was now, his head tilted, listening, tension radiating from him in waves.

His gaze had met hers and he'd said, "Those were rifle shots."

She'd shrugged. "I didn't hear anything."

"Have you ever heard gunfire of any kind?"

Grimacing, she admitted, "Only in movies."

"Well, this is the real thing, and I don't like it." His gaze swept out over the valley as if he could see through the trees.

Kat listened and heard some distant popping sounds. "Those are rifles?"

Mac nodded, swearing softly as he headed for the truck. "I'll be back in a little while. I have to find out what's going on."

"Why you?" she protested, putting out a hand to stop him. He didn't see the involuntary gesture, and she dropped her arm.

"Because it's my land, and my men wouldn't be shooting unless there was trouble. If it's not my men, it's another kind of trouble. Either way, I should be there."

"Okay." She trotted along behind him. "Let's go."

Mac came to a dead stop, the door half-open, studying her as he might a visitor from another planet. "Are you nuts?" he finally asked, his dark brows drawn together in a frown. "I have no idea what I'm going to find out there. For all I know, it could be a bunch of crazy survivalists who've decided to take over the country. There's no way in hell I'm taking you into something like that."

He stepped into the truck and slammed the door. The engine turned over and he stuck his head out of the window to issue a few last orders. "You're safe here, so don't go out on your own looking for those damn skunks. Relax. Read a book. Take a nap. Don't get into trouble. I'll be back as soon as I can."

And with another ferocious scowl, obviously intended to terrorize her into obeying orders, he put the truck in gear and tore across the meadow heading for the nearest road.

And that had been that.

Kat slipped the briefcase inside the tent and closed the flap, annoyed, both with herself and Mac. She was bored and, yes, just a tad nervous. The vast emptiness surrounding her wasn't a bit reassuring. She hadn't been on her own for any longer than it took to answer nature's call since she and Mac had begun this project. It hadn't occurred to her just how secure she felt with him and how much she depended on him. She wasn't thrilled with the realization.

She also wasn't able to follow his orders and relax. She didn't have a book that she wanted to read and was too edgy to take a nap.

"All right," she muttered. "I won't go looking for skunks, and I won't get into trouble, but I'm sure not going to sit around here twiddling my thumbs for the next few hours."

After strapping a webbed belt around the waist of her jeans, she attached a canteen of water and reached for her red baseball cap. As added insurance, she dropped a whistle in her shirt pocket. It was one of Mac's safety overkill items, but there was no harm in taking it along.

"I'm just going for a little walk," she informed her absent guardian. "Nothing to get steamed about, so just relax. Besides, I'll be back long before you get here."

There was nothing like a little exercise to settle the nerves, she decided a few minutes later, as she trotted down a grassy slope. For safety's sake—and with echoes of Mac's lectures ringing in her ears—she stuck to the edge of the clearing even though the trees beckoned, offering shady nooks and chattering birds.

The days were getting cooler, she thought with a clutch of dread. And they were passing by too quickly. The change was almost imperceptible, but it was there. The leaves were beginning to turn and there was a touch of frost at night.

One week.

Venturing closer to the tree line, she spotted a couple of dead logs and made a mental note to tell Mac. He had been right—of course. The areas around fallen trees, harboring nasty grubs and other such delicacies, worked as an irresistible lure to skunks.

Another small stream, twin to the one near their tent, sparkled like a silver sash a short distance ahead. Kat broke into a run, enjoying the smooth flex of muscles as she lengthened her stride. Leaping over a small outcrop of rocks, she reached the gurgling water just as two roly-poly forms tumbled out of the thickets in a brown blur, almost landing at her feet.

Cubs, she thought, entranced.

Pleasure turned to panic in the next instant. *Bear* cubs.

Kat's breath locked in her lungs as she cautiously began retreating. Rule number one in the wilderness—probably the only one she'd known before her indoctrination by Mac—was never, ever, get between a mama and her cubs. Especially if it was a grizzly and her cubs.

Slowly, backing away one cautious step at a time, Kat shifted her gaze between the wrestling cubs and the stand of trees behind them. A terrified glance to her right offered a hope of safety. More trees, she noted swiftly, surrounded by tall grass and bushes, a good place to hide. About ten yards away.

The cubs rolled closer, covering the distance at an alarming rate. Just short of colliding with her, they sat up, swiping at each other. One of them let out a bloodcurdling squall that sent Kat's heart to her throat.

A second later the mother charged out of the bushes with a roar. She was roughly a hundred yards away and ready for battle. Ears laid back, she reared on her hind legs and turned her head from side to side. She looked as big as a house and sounded like a freight train.

Kat broke into a run the instant the grizzly spotted her. She headed for the trees to her right, her head singing with fear. *Don't run...nine or ten feet tall...weight about a thousand pounds...can't climb trees*. Mac's words rang in her ears, but she still heard the bellow of the infuriated bear, the wailing cubs, and she felt the ground shudder from the impact of the grizzly charging behind her.

She tore across the grass into the thick brush. One tree, she prayed, just one perfect tree. With heavy branches, and tall enough to shelter her. Gasping for air, she broke into a clearing, flew up an incline and saw the answer to her prayer.

She left the ground in a flying leap, reaching upward for the branch that stretched out far above her head.

Tourists, Mac thought in disgust, turning the truck onto the dirt road that wound back toward the valley where he had left Kat. He had been prepared for World War III and, instead, had found two fathers teaching their sons how to pick off tomato cans. Lots of cans and lots of bullets.

He glanced at his watch and stepped on the gas. He'd been gone for over four hours, but he'd been lucky. The way sounds bounced off mountainsides and rolled down valleys, it could have taken a lot longer to find them.

But four hours away from Kat was time lost and, dammit, time was something they couldn't spare.

One week left.

His fingers tightened around the steering wheel. The minutes, hours and days were speeding by, and there was nothing he could do to stop them. Not a damn thing.

Kat was his for one more week. One miserable, glorious week. Mac took a deep breath and exhaled slowly. He wouldn't look beyond the next seven days.

He couldn't.

Besides, he had something more immediate to worry about. Kat. Alone. At camp.

He should have left her a gun, he thought with a frown. But, hell, what would she have done with it, shoot herself in the foot?

Of course, if he had taught her to use one, he could've left her without working himself up into a sweat.

Worrying about Kat had become second nature, he realized with irritation. He saw possibilities for disaster all around her. It wasn't reasonable. Hell, it wasn't even rational, but there it was.

For the last five years he hadn't dealt with such mind-numbing fears, he reminded himself. They had been peaceful years.

They had been calm.

Boring.

Lonely as hell.

He checked his watch again. If he went flat out, it would still take him another forty-five minutes. And what would Kat be doing during that time?

Anxiety knotted his stomach at the thought. She would follow his orders, he told himself, rubbing his belly. He'd get back and find her stretched out in the hammock. Or with her nose in a book. She wasn't the kind to go looking for trouble. She wouldn't wander too far away from the tent.

The thoughts were comforting; he wished he believed them. The knot in his belly grew colder, and the back of his neck prickled. He knew the signs too well to ignore them.

Something was wrong.

"Nice bear," Kat croaked, looking down at the berserk mother.

The grizzly had run through an admirable repertoire of snarling, roaring, throwing herself at the tree, slobbering and frothing at the mouth. Now she was having a temper tantrum.

The large pine had been a good choice, Kat reflected as she sat on a broad branch with her arms and legs wrapped around the trunk. Of course, she hadn't exactly chosen it; it had simply been there when she'd needed it. But it was healthy, deeply rooted and, apparently, the previous winter's high winds and snow had disposed of any weak branches.

Leaping for a limb had been a calculated risk, and Kat had known that, but it had been a chance. The rabid bear on her tail offered none at all. But the branch had been strong, and she had swung up, using her momentum to scale the next one, exactly as she did on the bars at the gym. The grizzly had hit the tree seconds later. Kat hadn't stopped climbing until she was a good twenty feet off the ground.

She hadn't escaped unscathed, of course. The bark had scraped a layer or two of skin from her palms. But raw hands were small potatoes compared to what the grizzly had planned.

Tuning out the snarls from below, Kat took a quick inventory. Her hat was gone, but she had a whistle, water and a body with all parts functioning. Not too bad for a novice. Of course, Mac would have had food in his pocket and a rope for rappelling. She gave a fatalistic shrug. What the heck, she could survive a missed meal, and even if she'd brought a rope, she didn't know how to rappel.

"Look," she said tentatively to the bear, "I'm not coming down, so you might as well go away. Your kids are bored silly, and my bottom is getting sore. I say we call it a draw. You scared me witless, and I got away."

With a roar of fury, the bear reared on her hind legs and systematically smashed all of the branches within reach. Circling the trunk, she batted at them, flinging them a good ten or twenty feet away. When they were all gone, she dug her claws into the tree and snarled up at Kat.

The shock of the breaking branches shuddered up the tree, reverberating against the insides of Kat's arms and legs. It was a strong tree, she reassured herself, tightening her hold. It had survived years of punishing weather; surely it could withstand the destructive antics of one bear.

Even a very angry, very determined bear.

As if to reinforce her thoughts, the grizzly began to rock against the pine. The tree swayed, and Kat tightened her hold. She wasn't especially alarmed. She knew that pines were flexible, swaying even in a gentle breeze.

After a few minutes of the relentless assault, she wasn't so certain. Sweat trickled down her temples when the tree gave an alarming groan.

Mac hit the brake and brought the truck to a skidding halt next to the tent. He was on the ground, heading for the tent before the motor died.

"Kat! Where are you?"

Something was wrong. He knew it in his gut. It was too damn quiet and she was nowhere in sight.

"*Kat?* Dammit, answer me!"

Mac checked inside the tent, then stalked back to the truck, swearing with quiet desperation. He hit three sharp blasts on the horn while he reached for his powerful binoculars. After sounding the horn again, he leaped to the hood of the truck and trained the glasses on the meadow, quartering the area, forcing himself to go slowly.

She wouldn't have gone into the woods without him. He had wrung that promise from her the first day. She wouldn't have done it. So she had to be somewhere....

He trained the binoculars straight ahead, following the grassy slope downward to the small stream. Kat could have been lured by the sparkle of water, he thought, allowing himself to hope. She loved the sound of it, frequently dipped her toes in the icy water, was convinced that she'd find gold. She wasn't a bit unhappy to settle for pretty rocks. There was a jar full of them in the tent.

Mac let his thoughts drift, deliberately avoiding the grim possibilities, as he backtracked along the stream, looking for her shoes. He followed the trail of water so intently that, for a moment, a flash of color in his peripheral vision didn't register.

He turned back slowly, moving his point of focus closer. There. He exhaled slowly, staring at Kat's baseball cap, a splash of red against the grass.

Mac lowered the glasses and jumped to the ground. He hit the horn again in three long, demanding blasts then reached for his rifle. He opened the shell, grabbed a coil of rope and headed for the stream at a dead run.

When he got there, he pulled up short, his gaze skimming over her hat to the mangled grass beyond.

Bears.

The evidence was as clear as it was terrifying—two cubs, rolling around, playing. The mother coming after them—and anyone near them.

Closing his eyes, Mac took a deep breath. When he opened them, he turned to follow the trail of trampled bushes and broken branches.

There was no blood. No blood. No blood. He chanted the words silently as an invisible talisman with every step he took. The trail was several hours old, he noted. Old enough for the bears to be at the other end of the valley, since they rarely stayed in one place for long.

When he was convinced his voice would work, he called her again. *"Kat? Dammit, answer me! Kat!"*

"Mac?" Her voice was soft, almost drowsy. And close by.

In a flash, the unadulterated fear that had consumed him turned to fury. He spun around, ready to throttle her. "Where are you?" he asked through clenched teeth.

"Up." Kat cleared her throat. "Here."

His gaze shifted upward, moving higher and higher, following the sound of her voice. Kat was straddling a thick limb, her legs dangling, looking down at him. She was pale but in one piece.

No blood.

"How the hell did you get up there?"

Kat winced at the softness of his voice. Her smile wobbled. "I think I flew."

Now that he knew she was safe, until he got his hands on her, Mac took the time to take in the rest of the scene. His gaze traveled down the trunk of the tree, stopping about ten feet from the bottom.

Savaged. That was the only word for it. The bear had torn off limbs and thrown them aside as if they'd weighed no more than toothpicks. She had gone at the tree as if she could tear it to pieces. Had actually slivered sections of it.

"How were you planning to get down?" he asked mildly, ignoring his churning stomach.

"The same way I got up—by way of the lower branches. But Mama Bear changed the game plan." She grinned at him, already feeling better. "I knew you'd have a rope. Were you a Boy Scout, by any chance?"

"Don't knock it," he advised, uncoiling the rope.

"Not me. I'm reaping all the benefits. How are we going to do this?"

Mac narrowed his eyes. "How's your balance up there?"

"Fine. No problem."

"Okay. I'll toss the rope over the limb. You grab it and make a knot in it. When you're—"

"What kind of knot?"

"Dammit, Kat." He scowled up at her. "I don't care. This isn't a test. A big, fat one that you can hang on to. When you're ready, hang on to the knot, slip over the side and I'll feed you more line until you're down."

"Okay." She leaned back against the trunk and smiled at him. "Let her rip." A second later, the rope looped up and fell neatly over the branch, almost in her lap. "Good shot," she said approvingly.

She knotted the rope, wincing when it scraped against her raw palms. Glancing down, she said, "Ready?"

Mac nodded. "Whenever you are."

She slid neatly off the side, letting him take her weight. Her feet had barely touched the ground when Mac threw the rope aside and pulled her into his arms. Held her with all his considerable strength and thought he might never let her go.

"Mac!" Her voice was breathless. "You're breaking my ribs." But her knees buckled, and she clung to him, trying to get closer.

"Don't ever do that to me again." His mouth was against her hair, his voice shaken.

She kissed his shoulder. "Never."

"Do you know how scared I was?" He didn't wait for an answer. "You weren't there. Not in the tent. Nowhere. And then I found your hat. Not you. Your damned hat. Surrounded by bear tracks."

She tightened her arms around his waist.

"I knew something was wrong," he said grimly. "I was two hours away from you, and I knew something was wrong."

"I'm okay," she soothed. "Once I got in the tree, I was fine."

"Once you got in the tree," he repeated in an expressionless voice. He stepped back to look at her, needing to see as well as feel. Touched her cheek with a shaking hand. Skimmed his fingers down her arms, clamping them around her wrists when she tried to put her hands behind her back.

He brought her hands up level with his chest, gazing at her torn palms.

"It wasn't the bear," Kat said hastily, breaking the charged silence. "I did it when I swung on the branch."

Mac opened his mouth, shut it and took a calming breath. He couldn't think of one civil or reasonable thing to say. She had almost been killed. That was the reality. She could talk about swinging through trees all she wanted, but that didn't change the fact that he hadn't been here to keep her out of trouble.

Touching the whistle through the fabric of her shirt pocket, he shook his head, anger building up again. "Did you think about using that? When I was calling for you might have been a good time."

"Oh, yeah." She looked down, brushed his fingers with hers. "I was. Really. But when the bear finally took off across the meadow, I was so relieved I..."

"You what?"

She shrugged. "I fell asleep."

"You—" Mac shook his head and turned away to collect the rope. He coiled it, giving her a fierce look when he unraveled the bloody knot. Draping an arm around her shoulder, he said, "Come on, let's go back and tend to your hands."

An hour later Kat tried to break through the barrier of silence that had fallen between them—a silence heavy with thoughts and unspoken words.

"Mac, I'll say this one more time." Kat scowled at him, waving her bandaged hands and hiding her concern. He hadn't said a word in the last hour. Once he'd cleaned and wrapped her hands, he had closed in, shut down.

She thumped the card table with the side of her hand. "Are you hearing me? It was nobody's fault. Not yours, not mine, not the bear's. It just happened. Things do. Life is like that. Sometimes all the plans and preparations in the world don't mean a damn thing."

Rather than look at his expressionless face, Kat closed her eyes. There was no point in being angry, she told herself. Mac wasn't using his silence as a weapon; he was simply dealing with things in his own way.

And so was she. In this case, her way was to talk, to deny what was so obvious. That they were having their affair. Their nonpermanent, short-term, great sex affair. But time was running out, and today's incident would only hasten the end.

One week.

And she wasn't angry. She could at least be honest about it.

What she was was scared.

Right down to her bones.

Eleven

Before dawn the next morning, she heard Mac's husky whisper.

"Doc?"

"Umm?" Kat stretched and snuggled into the curve of his body, her back to his chest. Mac's arm draped over her waist and his hand cupped her breast. It was almost dawn, and their bodies were still damp from making love.

"I think we'd better head back to the ranch when it gets light."

Kat stilled, not knowing if he said more. Not needing to know more. She concentrated on breathing as her heart stopped then slowly resumed its beating. Her head was filled with a buzzing sound as dark waves of panic swept through her. Panic and grief.

Oh, his statement sounded innocuous enough, but the hidden text was quite clear. It didn't need translating, and it didn't take a genius to know he was saying *It's over. It's time for you to go.* It was so soon, she thought, raising her bandaged hand to her lips.

Too soon.

She wasn't surprised, she reminded herself as she tentatively attempted to inhale. His reaction to yesterday's run-in with the bear had been warning enough. If she had needed more, his determination to start earlier last night and stay on the job until they'd collected the remaining blood samples she needed had been ample.

But that didn't lessen the pain.

She wasn't ready. She doubted if she would ever be ready to leave Mac.

From her heels to the top of her head, Kat felt his tension. And knew she was no better at hiding hers. When his arm tightened, pulling her closer, she blinked back the tears she refused to spill.

Mac had been honest with her from the beginning. He wasn't interested in marriage or a permanent arrangement. He offered an affair. With great sex. When it was over, she would leave and he would stay. Basic and simple.

She had known the parameters from the beginning—and had tacitly agreed to them by saying yes. So if she was hurt, she had no one to blame but herself, she told herself sternly. The only problem was, she had fallen in love—and had tried to convince herself that the rules no longer applied.

Okay. So she was wrong. They did apply.

Kat drew in a ragged breath, wincing at the shuddering sound it made when she released it. Along with the breath, she made herself a promise. She would go. Not just because she had agreed to, although that was a part of it, but because...

She blinked in the dark and realized that buried beneath the hope and tangled emotions, the decision had been made before she had opened her arms, her heart and her body to Mac. She would go because she deserved more than a man unwilling to make a commitment. Much more.

She would go back to the job that had always been such an important part of her life. Back to her family. And if she was lucky, someday a man would want her as more than a temporary lover. He would want a wife, a mother for his children. He would be a man who wanted her for all time, a man who loved her as much as she loved him.

So, yes, she would go, but not before she returned honesty for honesty.

Before she lost her nerve, she turned in his arms and laced her fingers through his hair. She felt his heartbeat pounding against her own, his body hard against her softness.

"Mac, I know what our agreement was, and I won't embarrass either of us by pretending that I don't. But while we're here together, in the dark, I need to tell you this."

She cleared her throat and rushed on. "This is about the hardest thing I've ever done, so don't interrupt. You don't have to do anything about it, just listen.

"I've fallen in love with you." Her fingers tightened in his hair. "I love you, I love your little brown-eyed boy, and I'm well on my way to loving your ranch."

When he made an involuntary sound, she shook her head. "No, don't. Let me finish. I can get a job out here, work in the area and commute. Or make a workplace behind the house. I've got enough money to finance my own studies, if I have to. I can do any of these things, and if you want me, I will."

Mac's arms tightened around her painfully, and his big body shuddered, but his words were clear and final. "No, Doc, you won't."

* * *

By the time they reached the ranch at mid-morning, Kat had established her goals. The first was to pack her car and leave—as quickly and painlessly as possible. She assumed that Mac would approve, but since they hadn't discussed the matter, she couldn't be certain. As far as that went, they had found very little to talk about. The three-hour drive had been awkward and uncomfortable.

Her second goal was to throw herself on her bed and have a good cry—as soon as she got to her condo. She was tired of smiling and trying to act as if nothing had changed. Tired of the invisible wall that had risen between them. Tired of holding back tears. A stiff upper lip was vastly overrated, she reflected as she slammed the truck door. All it did was lay the groundwork for a heart attack.

"Hey, you're back early!" Claude opened the back door, wiping his hands on a damp towel. "What've you done to your hands, girl? I got some of your favorite coffee cake in here, Kat. Come have a bite and tell me all about it."

Mac looked in her general direction. "Good idea," he said casually. "I'll unpack the truck first. You go on in."

"Cut me a big piece," she said, smiling at Claude. She lifted the cooler containing the blood samples out of its case and followed him.

"So where do you stand now?" Claude asked, pulling out a tea bag and dropping it in a large mug.

Kat looked around the refrigerator door. "I beg your pardon?"

He slid a slab of cake onto a saucer and took it to the table. Pointing a gnarled finger at the cooler she held, he said, "Blood samples. How many more do you need?"

"Oh, that. Believe it or not, we're finished."

"Good." Claude beamed at her. "Now maybe you can relax for a while. Just kick back and enjoy yourself." He darted another look at the bandages. "So what did you do to your hands?"

"I climbed a tree to avoid a bear," she said briefly, stirring her tea.

Claude narrowed his eyes then shrugged. He tapped the table by her plate. "Dig in, girl, you're lookin' kinda peaked. Has Mac been starvin' you out there?"

Kat dug in, knowing from experience that Claude would talk as long as she kept her mouth full. "How's Davy?" she asked when he began to run down.

Claude grinned. "He showed me how to play poker on the machine of his. Dang, that boy's a pistol with that stuff. That was a good idea you had, to stay a few days extra at the school and have someone work with him on the computer."

"Good. I thought he'd like it. They taught my nephew a lot."

"Yep, he'll be excited to see you. He's been working on some stuff, and he'll want to show off a bit."

"How's he doing in school?"

"A lot better since you and Mac talked to the principal and that teacher of his. A hell of a lot better."

"Good." Kat sipped at the strong tea and worried. Claude was no dummy. It wouldn't be long before he figured out that something was wrong. He'd badger her until she told him, and then he would try to drag Mac in the house so they could talk it to death. She'd rather face another grizzly than do that, she decided grimly. One major rejection a day was all she could handle.

On top of that, there was the problem of leaving. The idea of packing the car while Claude tried to change her mind and Mac silently looked on was too awful to consider. But if that was her only option, she'd do it. There was no way on earth she could spend another night here, not with her lover—ex-lover—playing the courteous host.

When Mac walked in, slamming the door behind him, she jumped and almost spilled her tea.

"Claude," he said abruptly, "I have to go into town. There's a breeders meeting. I was going to miss it, but as long as I'm back, there are some people I want to see. I won't be here for supper. Probably won't be back until ten or so." He turned, and for the first time that morning, his gaze met Kat's. "I'll see you later," he said deliberately.

Kat blinked and cupped the heavy mug with her sore hands. She took a long look at him when he turned back to face Claude. A last look. He had been running his hands through his hair, and his eyes were bleak. The sleeves of his blue work shirt were rolled up, the neck open in a vee. It was tucked into snug jeans that were soft and almost white from washing. He looked hard and handsome. Delicious. And…unhappy.

He started out the door, and she extended her hand, as if to touch him. When she realized what she was doing, she pulled it back, wrapping it around the mug, settling for a quiet, "Goodbye." Mac heard the husky whisper and swung around, his eyes narrowed, pinning her to the chair with the look.

Panicked, terrified he would stay, afraid he wouldn't, she softened the single word with a bright smile. "Have a nice trip."

Mac's sharp gaze remained on her face, as if he wanted to bore through her head and read her mind. "Later," he reminded her sharply. "Tonight."

Kat stared at the empty doorway until the sound of his truck faded in the distance. She had no idea how much time had passed when the touch of Claude's callused hand on hers brought her back to the present.

"You want to tell me what's goin' on?" he asked gently.

"Nothing." She let out her breath in a shaky sigh. "Absolutely nothing."

"Don't give me that, Kat with a *K*. Dammit, I saw you two together, and I'm old enough to know when—"

Kat squeezed his hand, almost breaking at his blustery concern. "You're right," she said shakily, "there was something. Something wonderful. But it's over, and I'm going home. Today. Before he gets back."

"Uh, Kat, maybe you're rushing things. Maybe if you gave it a little more time, you'd, uh…" Blinking at the fierce look she turned on him, he got to his feet and fiddled with the dish towel. Finally, tossing it over his shoulder, he said with painful honesty, "Mac's like the son I never had. He's a good man. He'd make you a good husband."

"Claude—"

"And Davy, he's a little corker, and he's crazy about you." He rubbed his hands on the sides of his baggy jeans and plowed on. "If you're worried about me being underfoot all the time, I could move out to the bunkhouse."

"Stop it, Claude!" Kat's voice broke. "Stop, please." Her eyes, when she looked at him, were bright with pain. "I told him I loved him. That I loved Davy. That I'd find a way to work here at the ranch."

She blinked back the burning tears that were threatening to fall. "It wasn't enough," she said flatly. "So I'm leaving. But I'll tell you one thing, Claude. If things had worked out, nothing would have made me happier than to have you as part of the family. As a grandfather to our children."

His watery smile almost broke her heart. When he opened his arms, she flew into them. They held each other, giving and receiving comfort, until Kat gave a shaky laugh and stepped back. "Don't you ever think of moving out, you hear me? You're the backbone of this family."

Impatiently brushing back her hair, she said, "I'm going to start packing. I want to spend some time with Davy before I go, and it'll be hard enough to say goodbye. I don't want him watching me haul things out to the car."

He brushed a finger across her cheek. "You sure about this?"

"Yeah." She nodded. "I'm sure."

"Then I'll bring the car to the back door."

Less than an hour later, Kat walked through the house looking for any stray personal belongings. She checked her watch and called to Claude, "I'm going to walk down the road and meet Davy. The school bus will be along any minute."

Davy spotted her as soon as he jumped off the bus. "Kat! Kat! Hi." He flung himself into her waiting arms, almost strangling her with his enthusiastic hug. "I didn't know you'd be back today."

"We didn't, either." Reluctantly, she let him slide to the ground and draped an arm around his shoulders as they walked toward the house.

Jumping from one event to another, Davy told her of all that was happening in his life. "And I'm the recess monitor this week," he ended triumphantly. "Miss Tedley says I'm a very valuable member of the class."

"Good for you." Veering to the right, she led him to the huge maple in the front yard, winding through its wide skirt of scarlet and gold leaves. "Davy, I need to talk to you. Can we sit down for a while?"

"Sure." He plopped down in a pile of crunchy leaves and looked at her expectantly. "What?"

Kat sat next to him and leaned back against the broad trunk, wishing he didn't look so eager, so certain she was the bearer of good news. Stalling, she looked around and finally said, "You live in a beautiful place, don't you, Davy?"

"Yeah, I guess." He gave her a puzzled glance. "Your house is pretty, too," he added politely.

"Thank you." She paused, wondering how she would get through the next few minutes, with Davy's curious gaze on her face. Picking up his hand, she brushed her fingertip across his palm. "That's part of what I want to talk about. My house. You know that I came here to do a job, don't you?"

He nodded. "The skunks."

"That's right. Well, I have all the blood samples I need, and—" she averted her gaze, looking over his shoulder, away from his trusting eyes "—now it's time for me to go home."

"You're *leaving?*" His stunned voice was almost more than she could bear.

She nodded, searching for words, finally settling for a half-truth. "I have to go back to work."

His fingers wrapped around hers, holding tight. When Kat finally risked looking down at him, Davy's chin was quivering.

"I thought you liked me," he said shakily.

Kat scooped him up in her lap, giving him a fierce hug. "I more than like you. I love you. More than any other boy I've ever known."

"I love you, too. Almost as much as Daddy and Claude."

"Thank you." She smoothed his hair back. "I'll always remember that."

"I thought that maybe you'd..." He stopped and gave her a doubtful look.

"I'd what?"

"You'd like to stay and be my mom," he finished in a rush.

"I would like that very much," she said gently. Suffocating with emotion, she struggled to breathe, trying to ease the pain in her heart. "But it's a little complicated. In order to be your mother, I'd have to marry your daddy."

Davy straightened, almost hitting her chin with his head. Excitement blazed in his brown eyes. "We'll talk to Daddy! I bet he'd like the idea."

I already did—and he didn't. Kat shook her head. "No, I don't think so. Adults don't do things that way."

"But—"

"I know, it's weird, but that's not the way it works." She gave him another hug and leaned back, waiting for the rest. He had more questions, hard ones, and she had to answer them honestly, without false hopes. She would not leave him with open wounds.

"Will you ever come back here?" he asked softly.

"I don't know." The silence stretched her nerves, but she held him and waited some more.

Finally he came up with the heartbreaker. "Will I ever see you again?"

Kat blinked and worked up a smile. "Oh, I hope so. In fact, if Claude and your daddy can spare you, I hope you'll come visit during your vacations."

"I don't know if I could," he said doubtfully. "I think they *would* miss me."

"I'm sure they would." She playfully flicked his earlobe with her finger. "It was just an idea."

Silence. It was eventually broken by his small voice. "Kat?"

"Umm?"

"I don't feel so good. Will you hold me for a while?"

"As long as you want, darling." Her arms tightened and she held him close. "As long as you want."

Claude was in the kitchen, cleaning cupboards—a despised task he reserved for working off his temper—when Mac walked in. He flicked a glance at the clock and said, "You're late."

"I know." Exhausted, Mac pulled out a chair and straddled it, resting his arms on the high back. "What a bitch of a day."

"Tell me about it." Claude banged a pot on the sink, taking pleasure in the jarring ring it sent around the room.

"Is Davy in bed?"

"Yep. Poor little kid was all worn out."

"Is Kat still up?"

"Probably."

"Where is she?"

Claude squinted at the clock again. "I'd say she's pretty close to Denver about now."

Mac stilled, his hands tightening on the chair until his knuckles whitened. "She's *gone?*"

"What did you expect? That she'd sit around here waiting for you to tell her she's not good enough for you? Again?"

"My God." Mac closed his eyes. His hand slowly clenched into a fist. "I never said that. I couldn't. She was—" He stopped. There was no way to explain the unexplainable. No way to describe his feelings for Kat.

"You might as well have," Claude said brusquely. "It all boils down to the same thing—you'd rather live with regrets than a woman who could bring some light back into this place."

Mac held up his hand. "Don't start."

"Hell, I'm not even warmed up yet. I've held my peace

all these years, but now I'm gonna say it. You're wrong, dead wrong."

"Claude—"

"Nope." He shook his head. "I've got a right to say it. I earned it by spending the day with two people whose hearts were breakin'. A boy who cried and a woman who didn't." He poured Mac a cup of coffee and handed it to him. "You weren't responsible for Cynthia's death. It was an accident, pure and simple. If you don't eventually get that through your hard head, you're gonna be one miserable bastard for the rest of your life."

"Dammit, Claude, I brought her out here." Mac got up so fast, the chair tipped over and fell.

"I don't recollect that you dragged her out here. I think she had something to say about it."

"She didn't know a damn thing about living on a ranch."

"And she didn't try to learn, did she?" Claude didn't wait for an answer. As far as he was concerned, it was long past time for honesty. "She was a nice girl, Mac, but that's what she was—a girl. A little spoiled, a lot willful. While you were gone, she took a horse you told her not to ride because she wasn't strong enough to control it. She took it out on a day a storm was coming in. She had to know about it. Hell, it was all over the TV and radio. Everybody knew."

He dropped a hand on Mac's shoulder, hurting for him. "No, son, it wasn't your fault. You ain't God. You never was and you never will be." He tightened his fingers in an affectionate squeeze. "I'm worn out from all the hurtin' around here. I'm goin' to bed now. See you in the mornin'."

When he reached the door, he gave a sigh and walked

back to Mac. "I forgot." He dug in his back pocket and pulled out a creased envelope. "She left this for you."

Mac looked down blindly at the envelope, taking a ragged breath. She was gone. Pain started in the vicinity of his heart and blossomed through his body. He hadn't known, he thought vaguely, that emptiness could hurt so much.

He heard Claude's door close and walked over to the table, sat down and carefully tore open the envelope. The note was brief, written on a piece of paper taken from her logbook.

My dearest cowboy,
I'm sorry I wasn't the right one for you. You deserve a happy ending. I can't leave without telling you that I will remember with joy the time we had together— remember and hold you in my heart until the day I die.

Kat

The words blurred and ran together. Mac sat at the table well into the night, holding the note in his hands.

Carole Heath, Kat's secretary, knocked on her boss's open door. "Are you busy?"

"No more than usual." Kat stretched and propped her elbows on her desk. It was large and edged with neatly stacked piles of paper. "What's up?"

"That's *my* question. I know I've been nagging you to get out more often, but I didn't think you'd resort to computer dating."

"What?" Kat blinked, not sure if her friend was serious.

Carole grinned. "That's what I said when this came in.

Frankly, my dear, you're slipping. This is either one very odd man, or you're into little boys these days.''

Kat's face lit up. ''One very special little boy.'' She extended her hand and waggled her fingers. ''Come on, give.''

Carole handed her the letter along with a moist, nut-studded brownie. ''Try this,'' she urged. ''It's just a little something I whipped up last night.''

Kat obediently nibbled while she pored over the letter.

Dear Kat,
You said I could use your E-mail so I did. I miss you.
Sorry I didn't write before. I didn't much feel like it.
Maybe I will visit after all. Claude is grumpy and
Daddy is mad. All the time. Both of them. School is
okay. The computer is fun. Write me. Love, Davy
XOXOXOXOXOXOXOXOXO p.s. That means hugs and
kisses.

''Great brownie,'' she said absently, rereading the letter. And a wonderful letter. She had waited, wondering if she would ever hear from him. And remembering the sad-eyed boy on the back porch, tears trickling down his cheeks as he'd waved goodbye, she had doubted.

''I haven't seen you look like that in a long time,'' Carole said thoughtfully. ''At least, not in the last couple of months, since you got back from that stupid skunk expedition slash vacation.''

Kat glanced up from the letter. ''Look like what?''

''Happy.''

''I've been busy.'' Kat scowled, knowing she sounded defensive.

''Yeah, yeah. You've been busy before, without losing weight and looking like you have soot beneath your eyes.''

"Come on, Carole. It's not that bad."

"Have you looked in a mirror lately?"

Kat didn't answer. Why bother? she thought. It was the truth. She looked like hell. She *felt* like hell. Not sick, just...tired. And for the first time since she'd walked into her custom-built lab Dan had provided for her, she had no zest for her job.

"Carole?"

"Hmm?"

"Have you heard any of the latest rumors making the rounds in the building?"

"You mean the ones that say Mr. Matlock is planning to start both an east- and west-coast division of this place? That he'll probably cannibalize this facility to get the others on their feet?"

"Yeah," Kat said dryly. "Those rumors."

"It's more than scuttlebutt, isn't it?" Carole pulled up a chair and sat, waiting expectantly.

Kat nodded. "He came by yesterday for a chat and asked me if I wanted to stay here or make a move."

"And you said...?"

"That I wanted to think about it. Well, now I have. I'm ready for a change, and Northern California might just be the answer. But I want to make sure you have a place to go before I take off."

"Kat." Carole made a tsking sound. "Don't you know that a proper executive jumps on the upward mobility track and never looks back at the falling bodies?"

"Then it's a good thing for you that I've never been a proper executive, isn't it?"

"Yeah." Carole grinned. "I guess it is." Her smile slowly fading, she said, "You've been a great boss, Kat, and even a better friend, so maybe it's time I come clean. I haven't found the corporate life all it's cracked up to be.

I've only stayed here because of you. My heart really belongs to—''

''Chocolate.'' Laughing, the two women said the word together.

''Are you really serious about opening a shop?'' Kat asked.

''Yep. Right here in town. All I need to do is find a sympathetic banker with a sweet tooth.''

Kat eyed her thoughtfully. ''How about taking a silent partner, instead?''

''You?'' Carole's eyes widened. ''Really?''

''Really.''

''I don't know.'' Her excitement faded. ''I wouldn't want to put you in a financial bind.''

''Carole,'' Kat said mildly, ''my grandfather, in addition to being brilliant, was filthy rich. Just because I came along with the Wainwright name, I got a bundle of what he left behind. I hate to see it just moldering away in an account.''

''God forbid,'' Carole said piously. ''Okay! I'll take it. But only at the going interest rate.''

Kat shook her head. ''At a fair rate. I'll take the rest in brownies.''

''Done.'' She reached over to shake hands with her new partner. ''So when do we break out of this place?''

''How about a month?'' Kat flipped through her calendar. ''That'll take us close to Christmas. It'll give you time to scout out a good location and maybe plan a grand opening for Valentine's Day.''

''What a mind.'' The budding entrepreneur allowed herself a few seconds to dream before sliding back into her secretarial persona. Looking around Kat's office, she groaned. ''In the meantime, we start packing.''

Mac stood in the open door and watched as a tidy redhead slapped a strip of tape on a box. She straightened, absently rubbed the small of her back and, looking around the office, shook her head in obvious discouragement. It wasn't hard to see why. The place looked like someone had dropped a bomb in it.

Carole turned around and gave a startled shriek. "My God." She held a hand to her heart. "You scared me." A sweeping glance took in his size and determined expression, and a wary look crept into her eyes. She edged behind Kat's desk, close to the telephone. "Who are you?"

"Mackenzie Ryder."

Carole blinked, instantly making the connection. "Davy's daddy?" Her smile all but blinded him. "That's quite a boy you have."

Mac's brows rose. "You know him?"

"I deliver his mail to Kat. Every day. Since it comes in on the computer, I also get to read it. How's Claude?"

"His arthritis is acting up," he said absently, looking at the room again. Tension settled in his neck as he took in the meaning of all the boxes. "Where's Kat?"

Carole grinned. "Flown the coop. Yesterday was her last day."

"She's *gone?*" Panic replaced the tension, and he wanted to shake some answers out of the smiling woman. "How do I get to her condo?"

"It's easy, if you can handle the storm out there."

"I'm used to chasing her through the snow," Mac said tersely.

Forty minutes later he pounded on Kat's front door. On the way up the walk he had passed a snow-covered For Sale sign, overlaid with a smaller one that said Sold. Leaning on the doorbell, he realized he'd forgotten to ask the redhead where Kat was going.

"Coming." Kat's voice filtered out through the intercom. "Be right there."

The door swung open, and Kat stood in a shaft of light blinking up at him. "Mac?"

"Who were you expecting?" God, she looked good. Too thin, too tired, but damn good.

"The pizza man," she said blankly. Fear leaped into her eyes. "Davy? Is he all right?"

"He's fine." Mac shrugged, masking his irritation. And his fear that she would slam the door in his face as soon as she recovered from her shock. "Would I be here if anything was the matter?"

She shook her head. "No, of course not."

"Kat, are you going to ask me in? It's damned cold out here."

"Oh. Yeah. Sure." She backed into the hallway, then further into the living room, when he stepped in and slammed the door.

It hurt, she thought, folding her arms across her chest. Seeing him brought it all back, felt as if someone had taken a knife to her nerve endings.

"I went to your office," he said abruptly. "Your secretary said you had left. And there's a Sold sign outside. What's going on, Kat?

She shrugged, "I thought it was time for a change."

"Where are you going?"

The doorbell rang while she considered her reply. "The pizza," she murmured.

Mac swore and turned back to the door, pulling out his wallet. Kat used the few seconds to pull herself together. When he came back, he dumped the box on the nearest table.

Moving to a chair a safe distance away, she stood behind it, using it as a shield. "Mac, what are you doing here?"

The bottom line again, he thought, as warm memories fought cold fear. Okay, if that's what she wanted, that's what she'd get. He'd forget the explanations, his plans to romance her. He'd forget everything except her.

"I came for you."

The blunt words rocked her, and her instinct was to run. She didn't want to hear about another affair, more great sex. She didn't want him to touch her, because she was very much afraid that if he did, she would agree to anything he offered.

"I don't think I understand." She cleared her throat. "In fact, I *know* I don't."

"Okay." He gave her a harassed look. "The bottom line. If you'll have me, I came to be your lover."

Kat closed her eyes.

"Your husband." His voice gentled to a whisper. "The father of your children. The grandfather of your grandchildren. But always, always, the man who loves you more than life itself."

Tears seeped out from under her lids and trickled down her cheeks. She buried her face in her hands and wept.

Mac looked at her, helpless in the face of her grief. Anger he could deal with, but not this silent, overwhelming anguish.

He scooped her up and sat on the couch, holding her close. "Doc, don't. I can't stand to see you cry. If you want, I'll go away." He wouldn't, but he thought it might calm her down. Instead, she clutched at his coat and cried harder.

"It's okay, sweetheart. It's okay." He patted her shoulder and made soothing sounds, torn by the shudders rippling through her slim body. "Look, I'm sorry. Whatever you want, I'll do." And this time, he realized, he meant it. He braced himself, saying, "So tell me what you want."

Kat lifted her face and wiped her eyes with the backs of her hands. "You," she choked. "Marriage. Your son. Claude. Children. My work, somehow, on the ranch. I want it all."

Relief weakened him, but he wrapped his arms around her and held tight. "Then that's what you'll have. What we'll have. Doc, I'm sorry. I was a fool."

She reared back, recovering fast. Her eyes flashed blue fire. "I know what you are. You're a stubborn blockhead, but you're *my* stubborn blockhead."

Relief fizzed through him. It was going to be okay. "Doc, I told myself I wouldn't rush you, but do you have a bed in this place?"

"Cowboy—" she leaned against him and pointed down the hall "—I thought you'd never ask."

"Nice bed."

"It is now." Kat kissed his chin. "It's been awfully lonely."

"Where were you going?" he asked abruptly, thinking of the For Sale sign out in front.

"I was heading west, Northern California to be exact. But yesterday I changed my mind."

"Oh?"

"I decided to go north, Wyoming to be exact. I was going to haunt you, wear you down. This is much nicer."

"I'll still worry," he said abruptly.

She patted his chest. "I know."

"I'll probably drive you crazy."

"For a while, I suppose." She didn't sound worried. "I plan to give you enough children to take some of the pressure off me."

"I love you."

"I know." She sighed and snuggled closer. "It's the only thing that kept me sane the last few months."

Leaning on his elbow, he looked down at her. "Are you happy?"

She nodded, touching his mouth with her fingertip. "Very. I can only think of one thing that would make me happier."

Worry darkened his eyes. "What?"

Kat grinned and reached for the bedside phone. "Let's call Davy."

* * * * *

Leanne Banks' exciting new mini-series
How To Catch a Princess
starts next month with
THE FIVE-MINUTE BRIDE
from
Silhouette Desire®

Here's a special sneak preview...

One

Beau lost the coin toss.

Jimmy's face split into a wide grin. "You get to address the little problem over there in the corner."

Beau Ramsey sighed and glanced around the nearly empty bar. Officially off duty, he was beginning to think he should wear a sign announcing that fact to the world. Right now he should be home nursing a beer watching the baseball game he'd taped earlier. "Technically this is a matter for the business owner to handle. You don't need the sheriff."

"She's drunk 'n' disorderly."

Beau glanced over at the little problem in the corner. "Drunk," he agreed. "Not necessarily disorderly."

"Just give her time," Jimmy said knowingly. "She's been knocking back tequilas for two hours.

She's either gonna get disorderly or she's gonna fall on her face.'' Jimmy gave a meaningful glance at his watch. ''It's closing time, and Thelma's waiting for me.''

Stifling a groan, Beau took another swallow of his beer and studied the little problem taking up space in The Happy Hour Bar. Pretty and blond, she was dressed in yards of white satin and lace that suspiciously resembled a wedding dress. From her painted nails to her satin pumps, she was a vision of feminine class. Her BMW was parked in the gravel lot. According to Jimmy, the only words she'd uttered had been ''Tequila, please,'' and ''Thank you.''

There was a story here, and Beau was convinced he didn't want to hear it. As a man who'd been surrounded by women his entire life, he could tell this one was in extreme distress. Unfortunately, as the primary lawman in the rural town of Ruxton, North Carolina, he was asked to address some pretty outrageous situations. ''You owe me for this one, Jimmy.''

Jimmy whipped his towel over the counter again. ''Put it on the tab.''

The tab was endless. Beau had been pulling Jimmy out of scrapes since elementary school. He rose from the stool and walked to her side. ''Excuse me, ma'am.''

Her blurred blue gaze rose to his. ''Yes, sir,'' she said in a husky voice.

Beau's lip twisted at the way her sexy tone mixed with the polite words. Her skin was flawless, her cheeks pink, her lips slightly parted. Her white dress drooped over one shoulder, revealing the shadow of her cleavage. Tendrils of blond hair escaped from what he guessed had once been a classic knot.

A dozen questions came to mind, starting with "Why aren't you in the honeymoon suite of a hotel with some lucky man?" and "Who's the poor sap that isn't going to see what's underneath all that lace?"

A shot of pure masculine curiosity thudded through his veins. Deliberately lifting his gaze from her breasts, he cleared his throat. "It's closing time. Do you need to call someone to take you home?"

She wrinkled her brow. "Home?"

"Yes. You've had too much to drink, so you can't drive."

She looked around and swept the skirt of the dress to one side to lean closer to him, then whispered, "Are you suggesting that I'm drunk?"

If he lit a match near her mouth, her breath would probably set the place on fire. For an insane moment he suspected that in a different situation her mouth would set a man on fire. He stifled a curse.

"Yes," he finally said, noting the pink garter just above her knee. "I am."

"Oh, my." She bit her lip, and Beau felt a tinge of sympathy despite his ongoing vow to remain unaffected by women in distress. "Where am I?"

Beau's hopes sank. She was worse than he'd thought. "Ruxton, North Carolina."

She looked at him blankly.

"Where do you live?"

She shook her head vehemently, then clutched her forehead as if the movement had been painful. "I'm not ever going home again. Never, ever. Not in a million—''

Beau lifted his hands. "Fine, but you've got to stay somewhere tonight."

"Why can't I get a room here?"

"Because there aren't any rooms here, Miss—"

"Emily," she told him, in that soft sexy voice that threatened his neutrality. "My name is Emily."

"And your last name?"

She frowned for a long moment. "I'm not sure." She grimaced. "I've never had this much tequila before. My stomach hurts."

"That's not the only thing that's gonna hurt," he muttered. "Okay, let's get you out of here." He offered his hand.

Emily took it and rose unsteadily. The woman was too trusting, Beau thought with disapproval, but he supposed her judgment was impaired.

"Where you takin' her?" Jimmy asked as he opened the heavy wooden door.

"I don't know," Beau said darkly. "My sisters' houses are crammed full with kids. It'll either have to be my house or the jail."

Jimmy shook his head. "She don't look like the jailbird type."

Beau just swore as Emily leaned against him, the soft floral scent of her hair rising to his nostrils. He urged her into the quiet night toward his Jeep.

"Today was my wedding day."

"You don't say." Beau glanced at her and felt another sinking sensation. He wasn't surprised. A beautiful married woman. This was not his lucky night.

Emily nodded solemnly. "He was a doctor." Her face tightened. "But he loves somebody else, so I left. My mother will have to be sedated. I'm never going back. Never, ever."

"I had a clue you might have been coming or going to a wedding," he muttered. "Your dress."

Emily jerked to a stop and stared down at her long white dress in horror. "I'm still wearing my wedding dress," she whispered, as if she'd just realized that fact.

*Look for THE FIVE-MINUTE BRIDE
by Leanne Banks, coming to
Silhouette Desire®
in September 1997*

▼™SILHOUETTE
Desire

COMING NEXT MONTH

THE FIVE-MINUTE BRIDE   Leanne Banks

How To Catch a Princess

Beau Ramsey was keeping an eye on Emily St. Clair ever since she'd decided she was going to live footloose and fancy-free. If anyone was going to give sweet Emily a wedding night, it was going to be *him!*

HAVE BRIDE, NEED GROOM   Maureen Child

Nick Tarantelli hadn't planned on getting married to save a desperate woman from a legendary family curse. But he liked the look of his beautiful blushing bride...even if she was only temporary.

WEDDING FEVER   Susan Crosby

Maggie Walters challenged the secret agent who'd so calmly proposed to her—she said that someday he was going to fall in love with her. He had a feeling that she might be right!

A BABY FOR MUMMY   Sara Orwig

What point was there in being stranded with a beautiful woman who couldn't remember if she was single and available...or married and the proud mother of two little girls? One was fair game, the other out of bounds...

TEXAS MOON   Joan Elliott Pickart

Man of the Month and *Family Men*

Tux Bishop *knew* that trouble was stalking Nancy Shatner and he guessed that he must be supposed to protect her. There was no reason to suppose that he was destined to marry this woman in jeopardy...

MYSTERY MAN   Diana Palmer

Canton Rourke had come to Mexico to relax with his daughter, not to catch bandits, track kidnappers...or save his neighbour, Janine Curtis, from any other mess she landed herself in!

COMING NEXT MONTH FROM

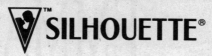
SILHOUETTE®

Sensation

A thrilling mix of passion, adventure and drama

HIDING JESSICA Alicia Scott
RENEGADE'S REDEMPTION Lindsay Longford
SURRENDER IN SILK Susan Mallery
THE LADY IN RED Linda Turner

Intrigue

Danger, deception and desire

HERO FOR HIRE Laura Kenner
FOR YOUR EYES ONLY Rebecca York
FEVER RISING Maggie Ferguson
THE DEFENDANT Gay Cameron

Special Edition

Satisfying romances packed with emotion

SEPARATED SISTERS Kaitlyn Gorton
ASHLEY'S REBEL Sherryl Woods
MARRY ME IN AMARILLO Celeste Hamilton
WAITING FOR NICK Nora Roberts
MONTANA LOVERS Jackie Merritt
DADDY OF THE HOUSE Diana Whitney

EMMA DARCY

*at her most daring with an
unforgettable tale of ruthless sacrifice
and single-minded seduction*

THE SECRETS WITHIN

When Tamara Vandlier learns that her mother is dying
she is elated—and returns to the family estate to
destroy her mother's few remaining months, in
return for her own ruined childhood. Loyalty turns
to open rivalry in this novel that explores the dark,
hidden secrets of two branches of a powerful
Australian family.

MIRA

**AVAILABLE IN PAPERBACK
FROM AUGUST 1997**

MARGOT DALTON

first Impression

Be *very* careful who you trust.

A child is missing and the only witness tells a chilling story of what he's 'seen'. Jackie Kaminsky has three choices. Dismiss the man as a handsome nutcase. Arrest him as the only suspect. Or believe him.

"Detective Jackie Kaminsky leads a cast of finely drawn characters... An engrossing read."
—*Publishers Weekly*

"Jackie Kaminsky is a great addition to the growing list of fictional detectives."
—*Romantic Times*

**AVAILABLE IN PAPERBACK
FROM AUGUST 1997**

LINDA HOWARD

ALMOST FOREVER

THEY PLAYED BY THEIR OWN RULES...

She didn't let any man close enough.

He didn't lrt anything get in the way of his job. But Max Conroy needed information, so he set out to seduce Claire Westbrook.

BUT RULES WERE MEANT TO BE BROKEN...

Now it was a more than a game of winners and losers. Now they were playing for the highest stakes of all.

AVAILABLE IN PAPERBACK FROM AUGUST 1997

FOUR FREE
specially selected
Desire™ novels
PLUS a Mystery Gift
when you return this page...

Return this coupon and we'll send you 4 Silhouette Desire® novels and a mystery gift absolutely FREE! We'll even pay the postage and packing for you.

We're making you this offer to introduce you to the benefits of the Reader Service™– FREE home delivery of brand-new Silhouette novels, at least a month before they are available in the shops, FREE gifts and a monthly Newsletter packed with information, competitions, author pages and lots more...

Accepting these FREE books and gift places you under no obligation to buy, you may cancel at any time, even after receiving just your free shipment. Simply complete the coupon below and send it to:

THE READER SERVICE, FREEPOST, CROYDON, SURREY, CR9 3WZ.

EIRE READERS PLEASE SEND COUPON TO: P.O. BOX 4546, DUBLIN 24.

NO STAMP NEEDED

Yes, please send me 4 free Silhouette Desire novels and a mystery gift. I understand that unless you hear from me, I will receive 6 superb new titles every month for just £2.40* each, postage and packing free. I am under no obligation to purchase any books and I may cancel or suspend my subscription at any time, but the free books and gift will be mine to keep in any case. (I am over 18 years of age)

D7YE

Ms/Mrs/Miss/Mr _____
BLOCK CAPS PLEASE

Address _____

_____

_____ Postcode _____

JASMINE CRESSWELL

Internationally-acclaimed Bestselling Author

SECRET SINS

The rich are different—they're deadly!

Judge Victor Rodier is a powerful and dangerous man. At the age of twenty-seven, Jessica Marie Pazmany is confronted with terrifying evidence that her real name is Liliana Rodier. A threat on her life prompts Jessica to seek an appointment with her father—a meeting she may live to regret.

AVAILABLE IN PAPERBACK FROM JULY 1997